PENGUIN BOOKS

SMALL TIMES

Russell Celyn Jones grew up in South Wales and now lives in London. He is the author of *Soldiers and Innocents*, which won the David Higham Prize for the Best First Novel of 1990 and the Welsh Arts Council Fiction Award. He has taught English at the University of Iowa, USA, and at Pentonville and Wandsworth prisons in London. His journalism and reviews have appeared in many newspapers and magazines, including the *Independent*, the *Observer* and the *Sunday Times*.

RUSSELL CELYN JONES

SMALL TIMES

PENGUIN BOOKS

PENGUIN BOOKS

Published by the Penguin Group
Penguin Books Ltd, 27 Wrights Lane, London W8 5TZ, England
Penguin Books USA Inc., 375 Hudson Street, New York, New York 10014, USA
Penguin Books Australia Ltd, Ringwood, Victoria, Australia
Penguin Books Canada Ltd, 10 Alcorn Avenue, Toronto, Ontario, Canada M4V 3B2
Penguin Books (NZ) Ltd, 182–190 Wairau Road, Auckland 10, New Zealand

Penguin Books Ltd, Registered Offices: Harmondsworth, Middlesex, England

First published by Viking 1992
Published in Penguin Books 1993
1 3 5 7 9 10 8 6 4 2

Printed in England by Clays Ltd, St Ives plc

This one's for
Dave Haines and Peter Llewelyn,
and for Rebecca Grace.

Thanks are due to: The Corporation of Yaddo for their generous support during the writing of this book; Caroline Dawnay, Philippa Gregory, Pascal Cariss, Carla Petschek, Angela Coyle, Penny Cherns, Peter Prince and Barbara Bayliss for their support and friendship. I would also like to acknowledge the help given me by Norman Hemmings, the dip squads of the British Transport and Metropolitan Police and to one or two others who would not appreciate being credited by name.

ONE

Harry Langland had been standing outside the Oxford Street department store for a touch too long. He kept buttoning and unbuttoning his suit jacket and drawing up his tie. He fell wide open to surveillance when the line of people to which he vaguely belonged tumbled into a 73 bus. He stared at the front page of his newspaper and the print refused to come to life. He looked at his watch, at the swing-doors to Selfridges, and felt the minutes sluicing through his skin.

Eventually the Chilean, Fernando, came out. Harry snapped his newspaper into a tight V-shape in his left hand, picked up his briefcase and began to walk. He collided gently with Fernando and felt the weight of a joey drop into the newspaper. Then he moved off in the opposite direction, holding *The Times* to his stomach. Covered by pedestrians, he plucked the joey out of the newspaper with two fingers of his right hand, held the briefcase against himself and tucked the paper under his right arm. Behind the briefcase he opened the joey and removed the cash, rolling the notes into his left trouser pocket. From his portside jacket pocket he drew out a man-sized Kleenex and wrapped the empty joey. He crossed to the south pavement and dropped it into a bin.

Outside a fish-bowl restaurant, Fernando, Jimmy and

1

Victor shunted up behind Harry. A floor-to-ceiling glass front afforded a view of the entire space inside. There were several bags lying on the floor and one dumped in the aisle between the tables.

Fernando and Jimmy Chaucer picked up on that and walked into the fish-bowl. Fernando stopped at the till and dropped pennies from heaven on the floor, then roared like a fool with coins around his feet, drawing everyone's attention. As waiters helped him gather the coins, Jimmy flooded the aisle, kicking the dummy along the floor. Through the window Harry saw him vanish into the toilet. When Fernando emerged to hold the ground outside the front door, Victor walked in and took his place at the till.

While Jimmy was out of sight, Harry watched Victor's performance with distinct unease. Jimmy had taken him on and Harry had met him for the first time earlier that day. There was something about Victor which made him feel pessimistic.

Jimmy emerged from the gents, shaving past Victor. He stepped onto the pavement and tacked east. Victor came out to brush against Fernando before heading west. Fernando met Harry on his island refuge in the middle of the busy road. Harry felt the hair on the back of Fernando's hand tickle his own. Harry gutted the joey in the usual way.

Jimmy, Victor and Fernando had gone in to spin a boutique, leaving Harry on his own again on the street. Oxford Street was a drought-cracked gulch, a town with no churches, and Harry never felt guilty working there. He felt the slippery bodies of consumers wiggle past his skin. They pushed and shoved and weaved around one another, little time bombs for hearts, mustering bad feelings and private tantrums, strangers bumping and grinding each other down, seeking redemption through spending; their worst fear to fail to make a purchase. If Harry got to their money before the department stores – did it really matter? At least his punters could return home with a resonant conversation piece. That's the way he looked at it, anyway. It didn't feel like he was doing them a favour, not exactly; it just didn't feel like a crime.

He must have given the whole thing too much thought, though, because Oxford Street began to oppress him in a melancholy way. He began to sink through a kelp-darkness, the air growing colder, inhaling the spent gas of men who had taken on the fathoms before him, in an attempt to get a finger-hold on sunken bullion glittering on the uneven bed. Sometimes this place was too much. Not just the danger of it, but the death rattle in the throats of all the minnows spending and stealing and shedding the same salty tears.

Harry spotted Jimmy strike a wallet in the boutique and surfaced so quickly his ears began to hurt. A jacket had been left unattended over the back of a chair, while its proprietor went off on a voyage down a full-length mirror in a new coat. Jimmy had covered his action with a Burberry raincoat draped over his arm and was now walking quietly to the door.

Harry folded the newspaper in his left hand. He received the pass and moved the joey to the other hand. Covered by the briefcase he removed the cash from the joey into his pocket then pulled a wad of tissue over the crocodile skin. With a certain theatricality, he wiped his nose with the tissue before throwing the bundle away.

Around noon they removed themselves from shops

and restaurants to bus stops. As they flexed their hands and shook out the static electricity, Jimmy fingered a couple of the competition – sullen black men in raincoats and caps. Bus stop dipping was a West Indian trick. The CID on the basis of that empirical evidence tended to see the world as black, at least at the bus stops. This gave a white firm, such as Harry and Co, a considerable advantage. Not that they relaxed surveillance. Jimmy claimed he could recognize any member of the dip squad working out of the Baker Street station. According to Jimmy he'd seen all their photographs in an album down his local pub. A south London 'family' had taken the snaps with a telephoto lens. Harry didn't know how reliable that was. It sounded like one of Jimmy's stories. Besides, dip squads were always changing personnel.

While Victor and Jimmy worked up to something, Fernando and Harry crossed the road to where eight people were waiting for a bus. When the bus pulled in, the queue stepped forward. The hydraulic doors hissed open and the last woman in the line unzipped her shoulder-bag. Fernando, muzzling in behind her, hooked the joey out of the bag, his body contracting like he was smothering a sneeze. Harry was given possession and walked away, turning off Oxford Street into Duke Street.

Outside the Ukrainian Catholic Church he ran into Fenton, an old poke from Bermondsey, who told Harry that the dip squad had joined forces with department store security, heating up the entire length of Oxford Street. 'It's ten degrees warmer round the corner.'

Harry relayed the news to Jimmy. 'Fenton said the whole street's under surveillance.'

'Fenton's trying to scare us off his patch.'

'I wouldn't put it past that bastard.'

'Well, you talked to him,' Victor said abruptly. 'Do we give him the benefit of the doubt?'

'I think we have to,' suggested Harry.

'It feels like lunchtime, anyway,' said Jimmy.

It is said that being perfectly dressed instils a contentment greater than any religion. The firm of pickpockets sitting in a packed Soho patisserie would bear it out. In Gianfranco Ferre and Armani suits, they sat elevated among students and artisans in squeaking leathers and ripped jeans, listening to their whorled conversations. At a glance they seemed perfectly serene, resting their hands on the white damask tablecloth as though in prayer. Cigarettes burned in an ashtray. Plates of half-eaten ham and cheese croissants and teacups had been pushed to the edge of the table. One pair of dexterous hands began fussily piling up pastry crumbs into a neat little pyramid.

To Harry, walking back from the toilet where he had been dividing the money, they looked a real picture. Had he been a painter instead of the kind of artist he was, he would have wanted to catch that expression of cool expectancy on their halcyon faces and finish their hands piled on the tablecloth in gold leaf.

They stared back at him in grave anticipation as he hitched up his suit jacket to avoid an unwanted crease and took the fourth chair. Harry stroked his burgundy silk tie and found a place for his briefcase next to Jimmy's Burberry folded under the table. With a calculator and *The Times* foreign exchange tables he had just estimated they had taken £2,000 in dollars, marks, francs, escudos, pesetas, lire and sterling. Without a word of conversation, he pay-rolled Fernando, Victor and Jimmy in three separate brown envelopes.

Through his clear-glass spectacles he explored the young and easy bodies in the room, who had not yet settled into any one lifetime role, burning up with strident dialogue. He smiled at Jimmy Chaucer playing mother, pouring tepid Earl Grey tea into a fresh cup. Jimmy was a hereditary dipper from South London, trained by his father in the craft. In close-up, Jimmy, circa twenty-eight, looked a corpulent schoolboy. Like a babysitter, a librarian. He just didn't look guilty. The perfect countenance for a pickpocket.

Jimmy nodded at one of the plates. 'You didn't eat your fucking croissant.'

'I'm not hungry.'

'Don't go to work on an empty stomach, Harry. Don't spoil it for us.'

'I had an Egg McMuffin on special at McDonald's for breakfast. I'm not hungry.'

'You've got to eat regularly. If you fade out on us …'

Harry stopped listening. He was watching Fernando tuck away his share of the morning's cash into a stack of stamped white envelopes with the same address in Chile written on each one. Fernando had Jimmy's innocence: rosy complexion, moist lips and the fixed smile of a child. His suit was one size too large and his neck hair crawled over the top of his shirt collar. There were so many Chilean pickpockets flocking the city all summer, that the customs at Heathrow had been told to pull over any triumvirates of Latin men arriving in Italian suits. Fernando had got in by flying alone from Santiago to Rome, picking up false EEC identification there and crossing to England by boat. Harry glanced at him licking his envelopes and acknowledged a natural talent.

Fernando was keeping a careful watch on other punters in the patisserie, on a man coughing at the next table. 'Everyone here has asthma, I think. In Chile I look up to the sky when I go every places.'

Somewhere along the line Fernando had attended dip school. Harry deduced this for himself, based on the tiny scars at the end of Fernando's fingers. Instructors sewed razor blades inside bags for the students to practise on in Chilean dip schools. Harry could think like a detective when he put his mind to it.

A pretty Italian waitress brought over a dessert menu and handed it to Harry. His looks had done a job on her. Pale skin and angular features contrasted with his head of black curly hair, like his white Jermyn Street collar against the dark cloth of his suit. A shop light sparkled in his spectacles, hiding the story in his eyes. He shaped his mouth into a humorous curve and waved away the menu. The waitress sauntered off disappointed.

Victor suddenly crushed a fly on the tablecloth with his fist. The force shook the crockery and made Harry jump. The sight of the squashed fly on the white cloth set Fernando's memory in motion. 'When I am in prison for five year I have only one room with nobody. In the summer I kill all the flies. I hate so much the flies. Many many flies and I try to kill them. Then in winter they all go and I miss them. They only life apart from me.'

Victor leaned back on his chair like a meat stone, trying to stare out Harry. 'You live near Broadway market, right?' Victor suggested.

'Wrong,' said Harry.

'Then why do I think that? I know why it is. You know Eddie the Shark. He lives near there.'

'Wrong again.'

'Yeah, you know him. The little poke with protruding bottom teeth. The one who spits up his nostrils when he speaks.'

Harry stared at Victor's blue suit. Its expansive lapels were designed to draw attention to the man inside. And royal blue was the colour for advertising agencies. Charcoal grey was the colour for pickpockets – the colour of thin air. It seemed incongruous that Jimmy contracted him at all, until he remembered that Victor was married to his sister-in-law. Harry had only known Victor a couple of hours and was already developing a prejudice. All it took was one prolonged look at Victor for the day to feel like Friday-the-thirteenth.

Harry pulled Fernando's face towards him as they were walking out of the patisserie. 'You've got tomato ketchup all over your mouth.'

Fernando failed to understand, so Harry wiped his mouth for him on a tissue. Fernando did not flinch. 'Harry ... Harry ...' Fernando repeated the name with some difficulty. 'Is hard for me to say. No saint in Chile called Harry.'

As they headed off to an underground station, Fernando dropped his four envelopes of money in four different postboxes on the way. 'In Chile I have wife,' Fernando told Harry. 'She very mystery to me. My wife she say many romantic that I will cry.'

At 1400 hours, the firm entered an underground station. No one bought a ticket. It was safer not to buy a ticket than be caught with one in the wrong zone: a piece of evidence for a court. Jimmy reconnoitred the

Circle Line platform. He selected their first punters, an American couple dressed in plaid with matching sneakers, from Iowa or Idaho, who would naturally assume the English liked them, if not want to *be* them. They were the best. Victor shadowed Jimmy. Fernando and Harry spread out a little further away.

When the train approached, Harry was amused by the way the American lady turned into the wind to save her hair blowing out of shape. In a minute she'd have a lot more to worry about. The train rattled through the tunnel and the crowd shuffled forward, creating an empty corridor behind their backs. Victor and Jimmy flanked the couple, with Fernando floating ten feet away. Where Harry stood between the carriages was a door button encased in a black rubber disc. Harry leant on it, waiting for the doors to part. Passengers alighted and the crowd entered the train. The American behaved according to stereotype and let his wife on first. Harry palmed in the rubber button, shutting the doors of that one carriage, cutting the man off from his wife.

She was now inside, her hands pressed against the glass, her mouth open like a fish. His arms began to flay and his eyes darted. He opened his mouth to shout but any words he may have thought of stayed frozen to his tongue. Victor stepped up and locked his arm around the American's right bicep, reeling out advice in a firm authoritative voice. 'Come. Come this way. I can help her. Quickly.' For that second, Victor was the strongest contender for a solution. The American, who had travelled here because he believed the English invented propriety, looked ready to fall into Victor's arms. Jimmy went in and out of the man's plaid jacket pocket, working like a matador, shaving as close as possible to the punter without making bodily contact, blocking out gaps of light that could expose his technique.

Harry began to walk down the empty corridor, past the line of backs. Fernando turned a key low down on the side of the carriage which opened the doors. Victor gave the man a push into the embrace of his fractious wife. Fernando and Victor peeled off. Jimmy couriered the joey to Harry in fast motion. As he punched it into his hand, Harry felt the sharp prick of Jimmy's nails he'd filed down into points.

Harry went on through an exit, busily gutting the joey. He didn't bother wrapping this one. A suit walked past and Harry dropped the evidence into its side pocket.

Each piece of work was a carbon copy of the first. It was routine and never changed. Other firms used different techniques, such as chalking crosses on the backs of bags of careless punters alighting the up-escalators, for their colleagues to dip on the street. Jimmy picked out the punters, and nine times out of ten they proved sound. He was a good judge of character. For sheer reliability American tourists were the best. Fernando took over from Victor occasionally. His Spanish not only deepened the punter's confusion, but sabotaged the transport police's intelligence gathering. It was hot and torrid activity and very tiring, working so concentratedly in an airless place. They covered a lot of ground between platforms and turnstiles at various stations, moving targets being harder to hit.

At all times the firm reserved a little energy to keep an eye trained for plain-clothes police executing similar moves: holding back when a train came in, dodging between platforms, standing in the corridors between platforms, lingering on a platform where all trains went to the same destination. Dip squads travelled in pairs, dressed in bomber jackets and jeans. Occasionally they came disguised as winos, or pimp and hooker. They were good, but often something gave them away. Like a radio micro-receiver in the wino's ear, or a can of Pils lager in the hooker's hand. Jimmy did think he spotted two on the Northern Line around half past three. He let the others know by clicking his tongue, as though gee-ing up a horse. They got on different compartments of the same train and rode them out, whoever they were.

Jimmy and Fernando slumped against the doors of the train while Victor nodded off in the next carriage. Harry's briefcase and pockets were stuffed with curren-cies. They had been on the move all afternoon, never returning to the same station twice. Harry had over-heated. He sat down and wiped the perspiration off his neck and face with a towel from his briefcase. He sprayed Evian water over his eyes and powdered his hands in talc.

It was approaching the end of the day, Harry could feel it. Concentration slipped at such times. Jimmy was so whacked he asked Harry to take over the lead role as they alighted at Embankment. On the District Line Harry psyched himself up as Jimmy selected the target: two sunshine-handsomes in their early sixties.

As the train came in, Victor and Harry moved into formation. The American put his wife on first and Jimmy punched the carriage-door button. The doors began to close around her like a clam. Then it all went wrong. The American managed to get his shoe between the doors before they closed and was trying to pry them open with his fingers. It was a lost cause and they should have left it there. But Victor had started his routine, tugging on the man's arm. 'Come. Come this way. I can help her. Quickly.' But he was too independent and ignored Victor. Victor eye-balled Harry. He tried to get into his breast pocket but conditions were far from perfect and he smudged it. Harry left a huge space and someone saw what he was doing. Through the gap in the doors Harry heard the woman raise the hue and cry. 'Watch out, Marshall! That sonofabitch is in your pocket.' The American caught Harry's arm and held him in a powerful two-hand grip with his foot still stuck in the doors. Victor stopped pulling and pushed the old man instead. He fell against Harry and they both tumbled onto the platform. Victor ended the fiasco with a hard kick from his Gucci shoe. The man's silver head ricocheted off the door of the train. His hold relaxed and Harry quickly rolled out from under him.

Victor, Jimmy and Fernando had vanished. Harry ran along the platform away from raised voices and the sound of banging prison doors. He could feel a whole structure collapsing behind him, like a demolished chimney-stack falling his way. At the bottom of an escalator he looked around to see if he was clear and spotted two uniformed underground staff behind him, tipping forward on their toes, their mouths open with hostilities.

Sometimes the body takes over like an automatic pilot when the brain has sunk in blood. Fear can be a great organizer, arranging footfalls out of chaos. There was not a lot Harry could remember between the platform and the street. But he had made it out with the briefcase. In a shop door he removed a fold-up mackintosh, threw it over his suit and swapped his spectacles for sunglasses. Then he began to run. He struggled to identify his location on the hoof, his head swirling in fog. A great many people blocked his way and forced him into the road.

Within twenty minutes Harry was walking, slowly, along the tow-path of Regent's Canal at Edgware Road. It was natural for him to gravitate there when things went wrong. For Harry it was a therapeutic place. Oxford Street, the underground, had taken something out of him which the waterway replenished. Over the years, Harry had stamped out so many anxieties walking its eight-mile length that he felt an affinity to the grim, earth-brown water and bankside architecture. The canal cut through all the extremes of London: high life to low life, John Nash affluent houses to council estates on desultory marshes. Yet the canal itself remained uniform throughout. It was modest. It was small time. No important public buildings stood on its banks and it was outside the sphere of tourists' interest. It reminded Harry, in hard pursuit of modern goals, that some things will always be the same. The canal connected with the Thames, with the English Channel, with the Irish Sea. Harry was born and raised beside the Irish Sea. His life felt less episodic and more progressive when he walked along the tow-path.

An ice-cutter passed by, its engine popping and laughing. The man on the tiller had coal dust in his blond hair. Harry strained to see if he recognized him as one of the people who lived on their boats. Along with Harry, hundreds of people lived on barges in London, existing without telephones, electricity, running water. Living on the canal was a clear choice for Harry. Others were forced there by the dearth of cheap housing. At first they tended to know nothing of boats and canals. Gradually the life took hold of them until they were alienated from the city. Harry was sentimental about water but kept clear of these monochrome outsiders who threw all respectability to the wind to live on it. Boat people were no different from people living on land. They were just as treacherous and selfish, squabbling constantly over money. But the element of water went some way to compensate them. The conduit of dirty water flowed under their poverty like ointment. It was a healing floor.

Jimmy Chaucer lived in a three-storey council block of flats in Streatham. Harry walked up from the canal, caught a cab on Marylebone Road and gave the address. As the driver headed south via Marble Arch, Harry studied the pedestrians out of the cab window, all following one of the two paths available to every man – honesty or crime. He watched them milling around the audio-visual shops and hotel awnings, dedicated thieves and civilians, and could see no way of telling them apart. Harry had forfeited his place in the civilian world seven years ago, when it was still possible to finger a thief. Something in his demeanour or physical shape would give him away to a trained eye. Now they all dressed corporate. They fitted in, in a surface kind of way.

Harry opened the briefcase on his lap and creamed around a hundred pounds of foreign currency from the pile of notes inside. He put the money deep inside his socks.

At the block of flats in Streatham, Harry rang Jimmy's bell and spoke through the intercom. 'Victor's an asshole, Jimmy. He should have let that last one go.'

'He's here upstairs. Come and tell him yourself.' The lock was buzzed open and Harry vaulted up three flights of stairs to where Jimmy was standing in the open doorway, saying, 'Victor's married to my sister-in-law, Harry. I got to look after me own.'

Jimmy had recently bought his flat from the council and had stuffed it with stolen furniture. Reproduction Chippendale armchairs still had their price tags attached to impress visitors with how expensive they were. Victor was sitting on one of the Chippendales reading a woman's magazine and Fernando lay on the floor examining the head on a leopard-skin rug.

It was hard to breathe in there. The heat was cranked up for some reason and all the windows were sealed. Harry felt his skin prickling from the moment he arrived. Jimmy's wife was listening to the radio in the kitchen. Harry recognized a classic BBC radio voice. The world was safe as long as that radio was on. Harry liked to tune in to *Woman's Hour* when he had the time, to glean advice on how women thought about themselves.

Jimmy's petite young wife emerged from the kitchen with three cups of tea on a tray. She had a bit of Chinese in her, Harry thought. Black hair, porcelain skin turning yellow, slant eyes. 'I'm Jimmy's wife,' she confirmed. 'Would you like a cup of tea?'

'No thanks,' Harry replied.

As she closed the door of the kitchen behind her, Jimmy whispered, 'My wife, if I said to her, "Honey, I'm just popping out to rob a bank," she'd say, "Okay, love. I'll fix you a lunch." It worries me what would happen to her if something happened to me. She don't know any other life except looking after me.' Harry spread out the currencies on the table and turned on his pocket calculator. 'Her niece come around here the other day with a new boyfriend,' Jimmy continued. 'The boyfriend only turns out to be in the Old Bill, doesn't he! Can you believe that? She's got the missus' genes, I swear. She brings this policeman in here and smooches with him on that stolen couch while the wife is serving them beer in Lalique wine glasses.'

While estimating the sterling value of their money, Harry took stock of Jimmy's testimony. He imagined what it would be like having this kind of authority over his own woman. He toyed with the idea of going back to Burgess on the boat and laying it down square: 'Get in the galley and make me a sherry trifle.' Harry liked sherry trifle. It was the only good thing to ever come out of his mother's kitchen. But he thought again. Jimmy's wife was probably born in a scullery. There was no way he could rule over Burgess by talking to her in the same way. She was her own man.

'There's five thousand, two hundred quid here in various currencies. Thirteen hundred apiece and some loose change.'

Fernando stood up from the floor and produced more self-addressed envelopes.

'Nothing missing is there?' asked Victor. 'You've had this money a couple of hours.'

'That's your fault, chum. We were one step short from getting caught. You should have let the old man go when he had his foot in the door.'

'That's not what I asked you about,' said Victor.

'I tell you what, why don't you and I go outside now and try and work this out in private?' Harry stood up. Victor, who seemed surprised that he'd made a challenge, squared up to him in a boyish fashion.

'Sit down!' Jimmy poked Victor in the chest. 'Harry, what is fucking wrong with you? Victor made a mistake.

It happens. You too, Victor. Sit fucking down! If I can't trust Harry, then I can't trust my wife.'

They all sat down and nobody said anything until Fernando cleared the air. 'It is very silence here, like the country.' He paused. 'I never understood the country.'

Jimmy saw Harry out to the front door. He saluted him from the street. 'Count me out from now on, Jimmy.'

'Over fuck all?'

'I want out.'

'We're only going to do another couple of weeks here, then go over on the boat. Do a season in Europe. You'll love Paris, Harry. The metro's air-conditioned.'

'No thanks.'

'Oh, come on! You're not going to work on your own.'

'I want out.'

'You've put me in an awkward position. Who's going to take over from you at a moment's notice?' Jimmy paused. 'You quit too easily, Harry. What's the matter with you?'

'I'll see you, Jimmy.' Harry started walking.

'Be lucky.' Jimmy grinned sadly.

He caught a bus a short walk away from Jimmy's and sat downstairs, its sole passenger. He opened the briefcase to retrieve his calculator and his share of the money. In among the towel and his mackintosh was an ox-blood leather joey he had failed to jettison. Harry went quarrying for the cash. There were so many compartments to the purse he had to pull it practically apart. He started sifting through the pile of personal effects. Blood donor card, credit card receipts for £1,800 and £972 – *sweet!* – an acupuncturist's appointment card, a receipt for Harrods' Food Hall. He dredged up an Equity ID card belonging to Gabrielle Scott, a BBC TV entry pass and an invitation to Sir Peter Hall's birthday party.

Harry was curious. He held up a page torn from a theatre programme which listed the credits of this actress, Gabrielle Scott. She'd been in fucking everything. From her photograph he could see she was quite a looker. Newspaper reviews had been scissored out and stuffed into the joey. Harry skimmed the pages: 'The incomparable Gabrielle Scott invests her greatness in Lope de Vega's small-life heroine. Scott's performance is an enriching experience ... unexpectedly uplifting ... she is a cause for celebration.' No ordinary actress, it seemed.

Finally he discovered the cash, around £400 in sterling. Bingo! This was an exceptional haul. If everyone inhabiting theatres carried this kind of stash, then why hadn't he known of it before? He was missing out on a gold mine. He would do well to include such places in his repertoire. It had never occurred to him to work in theatres, because they were outside his cultural experience. But not any longer. He intended to check in to one tomorrow, or soon after. The Vaudeville was on the Strand, and the Strand was on his beat.

Harry folded the programme notes, the money and the joey into his pocket and bundled what he didn't want to keep into the briefcase.

As the bus crossed Vauxhall Bridge he walked to the back and stood on the platform. With an underarm swing he flung the briefcase out of the bus. The case cleared the wall of the bridge and plunged into the Thames below.

TWO

Unlike his colleague Jimmy Chaucer, Harry Langland was not a hereditary London pickpocket. He was the only child of farm labourers from a western peninsula, where people were chained to the soil, dulled by certainty of season, frozen in the shadow of the church spire. Unless you worked the land, the land had no use for you. Harry never wanted to work the land. His adolescence had been spent in a state of breathlessness from doing nothing, from the landscape doing nothing, its only changes seasonal, otherwise invisible to the naked eye. He used to sit in fields screwing up his eyes, wishing the ground to crack open like a chrysalis and give life to people undertaking adventurous projects.

At eighteen he attended technical college with the intention of becoming a building engineer. But there was nothing as intrinsically exciting about building technology as there was in theft. He stole from locker-rooms in the college and progressed to coats and bags left in the staff room while teachers were in class. Stealing lent gravity to his monotonous rural life and went some way to assuage the loneliness of being an only child.

The sea was his only friend and more reliable than family. He messed around on boats and created an elaborate fantasy of an older brother away in the Merchant Navy who was going to return one day and put

Harry back on the rails. This fantasy began to justify the theft.

Harry was eventually caught by the college principal. To escape the consequences he ran away to London for the weekend and never returned. In the years that followed no one ever came looking for him, or cried for him. There was nothing for him to be nostalgic about. Nothing at all.

All he could discern of London at first was its collage of sounds and fast-moving objects: vague, violent, compelling. He wandered around the city, looking through office windows at attractively dressed people laughing and smoking cigarettes. In Chelsea he was pushed off the pavement by women. He followed an Iranian into a jewellers and watched him spend £40,000. All of which convinced him that better men were engendered by diesel fumes. The city was toxic, but filled with people fighting to live. And the fight for life was a celebration of awareness.

He slept for a while in Lincoln's Inn Fields and met a tramp who studied eastern religions in Westminster Public Library. He told Harry how Buddhists believe we choose our parents. That convinced Harry he should reject his parents outright. So he started over again there in London. The hydraulic squeal of brakes, sirens, the banging and scraping of construction sites became the new music in his ears, replacing the song of seagulls chasing the plough.

He rented a bedsit in Camden and began stealing handbags, briefcases to pay the rent. Not really a home, not exactly ... but there were possibilities. And possibilities, not certainties, inspired Harry. He'd had it up to there with certainties.

After a few months in London Harry met a young woman on the underground. What initially attracted him was the open satchel hanging off her shoulder. A turquoise purse sat on top of other miscellany. He followed her down an escalator onto a crowded platform. As she moved forward with the crowd when the train came in, Harry entered the work space behind their backs and dipped her bag. From inside the carriage a short stout passenger barged his way forward into the platform crowd. Several people fell back like dominoes, including Harry's quarry into his arms. She would have fallen over had he not been there. And it might have been wiser to let her drop, taking all the facts into consideration. But then Harry was a Celt, so he had some compassion. Regaining her balance, the woman turned round and transmitted a fresh, shy smile and transformed the city for him. He breathed in and cleared his head.

She was about twenty years old and already in decline. Her skin was creasing on her forehead, her light brown hair shocked into premature greyness. She was dressed badly, in frayed tracksuit pants and a shrunken cardigan which smelled of wood smoke.

As she began to board the train Harry decided he didn't want to keep her purse. He followed her into the carriage where she took a seat between two other passengers. The doors closed and Harry found himself taking an unscheduled journey.

She got off at Paddington, pursued by Harry along the platform. She reached the street and he lost the opportunity to replace the joey. The rhythm of her walk had a mesmerizing effect. She moved like a sailor on land. He stayed on her tail following other instincts.

She left the pavement to walk under a bridge, doubling back on herself along the tow-path of the canal. He wondered why all things led to water. Now Harry didn't know what to do. He kept following for want of a better idea. At Marylebone she veered off along an arm of the canal into a large basin. Empty warehouses, derelict wharves shouldered the water, itself a dead end depository for a ton of flotsam. She ducked under a ramp in the tow-path and disappeared into one of the warehouses.

Harry let a few moments pass before following her. The ramp was so low it forced him to crawl along the edge of a waterborne entrance. He stood up slowly inside the warehouse. A weak light filtered through a latticed ceiling onto the water. Around this interior basin ran a cobblestone ledge. He had crawled into a deserted tomb of a place where barges had once unloaded their cargoes. He could see no one, but heard voices whispering, terse and eerie, with outbreaks of laughter spanking the surface of the water. He peered into the deep storage vaults in the walls, positioned himself so whoever was in there could see him.

The laughter and whispering drained away. The only sound was of water dripping into the basin. Then the invisible became tangible threats. Bottles rolled on concrete, newspaper was torn as three men tumbled out into the twilight and surrounded him. They were tall, wide-shouldered, with stitched faces – around the fifty-year age bracket. Harry's legs were kicked from under him and he fell across a mooring ring.

Their air was boozy but they were not push-over drunk. Perhaps if Harry'd come around later they might have been. But it was only mid-morning and no one knew he was down there. Perhaps no one knew *they* were down there. They could do their worst to him and take all day about it. Harry began to shake violently.

The woman stepped out of the vault and stared at him. She gave off the distinct feeling of being the one in charge. He pulled out her purse from his pocket and offered it to her in his outstretched hand. She looked at him wryly and began to smile. 'You dropped this,' he scrambled.

She took the purse and opened the clasp to show him it was empty. There wasn't even a credit card.

Harry was offered the communal bottle. 'Have a drink on me,' she said, 'for your trouble.' As his survival seemed to depend on it, he accepted her offer. He sat in the vault on duckboards and blankets, drinking warm sherry, not knowing when he'd get out again. He could not see their faces, could only hear the men's grumbling, swallowing and snatching of the bottle. Her voice roamed widely and sometimes her white teeth flashed in the dark.

She told Harry she'd come to London at fifteen, arriving at King's Cross with five pounds in her pocket and a carrier bag of clothes. She sat on a bench in the station concourse, wondering how to transfer to the next stage of the adventure. A sympathetic citizen came along and was kind. He gave her cigarettes, then a shoulder to cry on, finally a place to stay for the night. In no time at all, he had her working for him around that same station, with the rest of London lying fallow beyond the Euston Road.

What kind of work this was she didn't explain, except to say it wasn't prostitution nor drug related but that her 'pastor' broke four of her fingers with a steel wrench. She held out her hands for Harry to feel in the dark.

'Touch them,' she said. Her skin was rough like fish-scales, her fingers crooked and bumpy.

Each time her pastor 'did my brain in' he would break down and cry. 'When I had to go to hospital after he'd kicked me in the head I thought he'd never stop weeping. Talk about cry me a river.' During the night she slipped out of her hospital bed and headed north to the canal. She walked along the tow-path and found the warehouse. She crawled under the ramp and fell asleep on the cobblestones. She did not know that three men lived there already. They found her in the morning, their own Sleeping Beauty. For five days they did what they could, keeping her warm, taking it in turns to check on her. When she finally woke they fed her with bread and milk, like you would an injured sparrow.

She had continued to hide under the warehouse ever since. The people who had controlled her life for so long were still dangerous. They had no compassion. It was a rule of theirs to hunt down any 'daughter' who deserted, even if it took a lifetime to find her. (She implied more than once that they were a religious sect.) But she felt safe there, in a dark vault with a Scotsman, an Irishman and a Welshman who had closed everything down on themselves with alcohol. 'They watch over me,' she said.

Her name was Burgess. Just Burgess. Her partial name was all she had to hide herself from violent evangelists, social workers, police and other such people she didn't care for, snooping around. No postman ever came to her address, so she didn't actually need a full name.

Whenever he was feeling scorched from relentless crime Harry checked in with Burgess. She was the only woman he had met in London. They'd sit in one of the vaults drinking the liquor he'd brought, studying each other's face in the glow of cigarettes. He made a couple of thwarted advances when the drunks were out of the warehouse or out of their minds, until she finally gave in and absorbed him like blotting-paper.

After a year in London he was caught in the Russell Hotel stealing a briefcase off the floor under the concierge's desk. In court the judge was asked to take two other offences into consideration. The judge, responding to the 'plague of pickpockets' appearing in London, sentenced Harry to eighteen months. Overnight he learnt the difference between country and city life. If you failed in the country there was a lot more soft ground to break your fall. Burgess never visited him the whole time he was inside. He assumed she was too scared to make a trip to an environment where the kind of man she'd known in the past could be found.

There was no union in prison between men of different walks of life. It was not an ecumenical place. It was not even forty days in the wilderness. The first three days were novel enough, but thereafter everyone began to repeat himself. Banged-up, blue-striped liars, re-creating their moment of glory in a bank raid, on a rooftop, in a pub brawl, did not know how to communicate. They talked in rambling monologues and fantasized. Prison began to look like the undoing of Harry Langland. His morale slid down with alarming speed.

Then he met Jimmy Chaucer. Jimmy helped shape Harry's attitude from amateur Celt to professional pickpocket. They rehearsed tricks in their cell. Jimmy showed him how to make his hands more flexible and later, on the out, what suits to wear. When Jimmy was released, Harry stood out as an inmate with no friends and started getting threatened by one or two of the hard men. So he looked around for a companion to replace Jimmy and settled for Denis O'Sullivan, a former nonce.

Nonces are the most despised inmates in prison. The only status a man has in gaol is the crime he committed. Murder is the outrage of the aristocracy. Burglars, fraudsters occupy the middle ground. Hereditary pickpockets like Jimmy Chaucer are held dear as cultural artefacts, in a class of their own. But sex offenders and grasses – the nonces – have no rank whatsoever. They have to go through every meal with a finger looking for ground glass. In Harry's HMP these Rule 43 inmates' cells were directly above his own. All night long a steady stream of laughter poured down from that landing, a sprinkling of immature giggles. It was the stolen music of children, and made men mad to hear it.

Occasionally an overlap occurred during slop-out and a nonce would get stranded on the landing as regular inmates appeared. Some men would try to do their worst in the short time they had. Drunks, muggers, sweet-shop thieves went in for that kind of thing to raise their own self-esteem, although Harry once saw a nonce killed on E wing by a man who'd murdered his wife. He beat the nonce over the head with a radio battery concealed inside a sock. His life sentence was doubled, so what did he care? Screws turn a blind eye to such episodes. It is something they can't do for themselves.

That was how Harry first saw Denis O'Sullivan, a tattooed Frankenstein fighting for his life on E wing. He was a Rule 43 inmate, serving time for attempted rape. Harry saw him kicked, punched and stabbed with mailbag needles welded into toothbrush handles. Nonces either fought like girls or not at all, so it was astonishing to see this one take out three of his assailants before the screws broke it up. Several weeks later Denis was released, having made a successful appeal against his conviction. Within a month he reappeared among the regular inmates on a four months' sentence for receiving stolen goods and beat up any stranded nonces he could get his hands on.

Harry let Denis know he'd seen him on the Rule 43 landing, blackmailing him into friendship. In return Harry listened to Denis, which for Denis was a new experience. Listening came easy to Harry, as a child who had been seen and not heard, with no siblings to commiserate. He made others feel that the gravity of their words weighed down his own, that what they said was important. Harry had realized a long time ago that people were only interested in themselves, and that nobody says anything until someone listens.

Denis told Harry all about his father beating him up as a kid. How he broke his arms with a cricket bat, then broke his mother's jaw for intervening. After each of these frenzied attacks, Mr O'Sullivan's two victims would sit in the kitchen with a Bible and repeat together, 'We're all Jesus! We're all Jesus here!' until the pain and the fear went away.

When he was eleven Denis hit his father across the head with a fire poker. The wound required eleven stitches, one for each of Denis's tender years. From what Harry could gather, grounding his father was the greatest familial joy Denis had ever experienced. Every fight he'd started since was an attempt to recapture that joy. When he saw his father's face in an opponent's he could never be beaten, or whenever any other inmate tried to assault his best friend Harry, the only man who ever listened to him, Denis would work him over as a way of ratifying the friendship. Sometimes Denis would promote situations to get Harry threatened, so he could confirm his loyalty. No one quite loved Harry like Denis O'Sullivan.

On the day of Harry's release from prison the first thing he did was seek out the atmosphere of water. After an hour's ramble along the canal tow-path, he reached Marylebone basin, hoping to find Burgess in the same place.

As he approached the basin, Harry was astounded to see, rising out of the pallid enclave of warehouses, a premonition of its new future. Embryonic shapes of offices, hotel and flats were taking shape. Most impressive was a shopping mall made of glass and white steel, soon to be full of people wandering around dazzled by light and consumer goods, not quite certain why they had come in the first place.

All this had gone up in the time he'd been away. The cluster of wharf, warehouse, gasometer, was having its last stretch in the clouds. In had come cranes, scaffolding, smoked glass. Soon it would be buzzing with rich portents, rich people.

The only original building still standing on the site was Burgess's warehouse. Formally a store for Arctic ice one hundred years ago, it was now destined for an apartment complex. Hard hat construction workers scuttled across scaffolding. Harry could see two- and three-bedroom flats taking shape inside. Each bathroom had a porthole window, with marble pillars in the lounge and windows stretching from floor to ceiling.

Drowsy with visions, Harry dragged his limbs into

the building, doubting he'd find Burgess there any more. Under the latticed ceiling he saw something else that was new: a rusting hull and superstructure of a barge sitting in the water. The air was laced with acrid smoke issuing from a chimney in its roof.

Harry climbed on the deck and entered the front cabin. Burgess was sitting on an old car-seat inside, with fifty feet of hollow steel at her back piled high with timber, paint, power tools, old clothes. Sleeping on a stack of newspapers was a baby. As soon as she recognized Harry, Burgess laughed her greeting. 'What have you got to laugh about?' Harry said. 'Where'd that baby come from?'

'The guys out there delivered her for me. Three men blasted by drink became midwives when they had to be. It was like a miracle.'

'Which one is the father?'

She smiled densely at Harry. 'She hasn't got a father. Or maybe she's got two.' Burgess had a lazy eye. One held a fix on you while the other took a little extra time to focus and join in. Once in her sights it wasn't easy getting away. Harry could not squirm out of it, despite himself. 'And this is my ark you're standing in.' She lay on a foam-rubber mattress beside the baby.

'Why an ark?' Harry asked, playing it loose.

'Because this place is about to fall. There's nothing here for me any more.'

Harry sat next to the baby sleeping with her arms outstretched. He still couldn't get over the boat, which Burgess had found partially sunken in the canal. With a vision of its past life she set about raising it, bailing out the water with a dustbin. She punted it over to where a few gypsies were moored and they had lent her a battery and helped her strip down the engine to get it going.

When he probed more about the avatar in the cot, she grew vague. 'Maida Hill tunnel is two hundred and seventy two yards long and takes one and a half minutes to get through at 4 mph. The headlamp strapped to the front reflects the roof of the tunnel in the water. It makes you feel you're floating in air. Once you enter a tunnel you never want it to end. I was standing at the tiller when I felt my skirt being lifted up from behind. The chimney smoke was drifting forward through the head-lamp beam. In the smoke were green dragonflies and the sun shone in the tunnel mouth on clear blue water. The engine sounded like a baby crying. Then the whole thing popped, like a balloon. Stars came out in the daylight and I had a thirst so powerful it seemed to come from the back of my brain. No one was there when I came out of the tunnel. Don't know where he went. But one and a half minutes isn't very good for a man, in terms of restraint, is it?

'I've been a little destructive in my life, as you know,' she continued, 'but I call those bad times adventures now, now I've got this little child. She's helped me get my head together.' She smiled at her thoughts. 'All I want is something protective around us. Like a home, but not a house. I don't want to live alongside the kind of people who elbow you off the pavement. Right above our heads they're building homes for those kind of people. They're welcome to the place. I worked it out. This boat cost me nothing, and it will cost me nothing to fit out.'

'Where have you learnt to fit out a boat?'

'I didn't learn anything. I just found that I could do it. When you have to, you know what to do.'

'What do you call the baby?'

'Simmy.'

With baby Simmy hinged to her breast, Burgess took Harry on a tour of the boat. They couldn't get from one end to the other without climbing. Stocked up beyond the first bulkhead were new and old timber, plywood, zinc and brass screws, plumbing gear, copper pipes and concrete paving-stones. She had stolen the material and power tools from the site after the men had gone in the evening.

In the aft of the boat she explained how the boatman's cabin would look one day, with a Torglow solid fuel stove and back boiler, hanging brass kettles, a twin berth, a hinged table that doubled as a cupboard door; everything in reach from a sitting position. A snug little nest six foot by ten with the feel of water lapping around your back. Like a womb, there would be no space to move around, nor accommodation for the outside world. In the middle of the boat she had chalked out the galley's shape, where the cooker and fridge – when she could afford to buy them – and sink and cupboards would lie in an L-shaped configuration. Next to the galley would be the bathroom with the central corridor running between the shower and WC. Harry struggled hard to envisage the completed vessel. Burgess had the only blueprint and that was in her head. The engine was a Russell Newbery DM2, built in 1932. 'It's got a piston stroke of twelve inches in every revolution,' she said. 'Low rpm. That makes quite a difference to the wear and tear of the thing. It's a lovely piece of engineering.'

That night, Burgess and Harry slept together on the foam-rubber mattress with the baby at their head. The ground listed discernibly one way and then the other. After two years of abstinence from one another, Harry and Burgess reclaimed old territory in a passionate embrace. The baby slept soundly, letting them get on with it.

He refamiliarized himself with her body. She still felt like a child in his arms, for all her experience; like a porcelain Alice innocent of the ways of men. He ran his hand over her breasts and found that the baby had sucked the form and substance out of them. They stopped short of intercourse and Harry was quite comfortable with that, since it inevitably brought trouble.

Harry stayed on at the boat. He returned there every night, after a day's thieving, and slept with Burgess. The boat was surrounded in the darkness by the three drunken tragedies sleeping fitfully in their cardboard skippers. Harry woke constantly to their weeping and contentious dreams. They were men with no hope. But if ever Burgess more than murmured in the night, he would have been a dead man. In Burgess all their lost aspirations were embodied. The only times they surfaced from that place was to go on errands for her and to beg. They pooled all their money for drink and never seemed to eat. They brawled and punched each other in weeping rages. Yet they were brothers too, determined to go out of the world together.

After Harry had been there a few weeks, Burgess started worrying him by talking of a relationship together. Harry lived for the day and pooh-poohed such nonsense, but unwittingly encouraged her aspirations by gradually bringing on board suits by Pierre Balmain, Dunhill, Kenzo and Hugo Boss. He hung the suits, along with a few Paul Smith shirts, in the boatman's cabin above a neat row of bench-made shoes.

Each night after he fell asleep he had the same nightmare that the boat was sinking.

'What do you do now, Harry?' she asked one morning as she fed Simmy on her breast. 'You still dipping?'

'With Jimmy. In a firm. We're going to Europe next summer.'

'That must be agony on the brain.'

'What d'you mean?'

'Wondering when you'll next get caught.'

'There's no way to avoid stress when you're earning a lot of money. It comes with the territory.'

'Steal it, you mean. You said earn, when what you mean is steal.'

'What's the difference?' As far as Harry was concerned this was a plutocracy and in a plutocracy the difference between stolen money and earned money was ambiguous.

'I was just correcting your English.'

'All I know is without money you don't have power and without power you don't have choices. Simple economics, Burgess.'

She sat the baby on her knee. Simmy looked at the open door in the front of the boat and then slowly her head turned to the other end, through a semi-circle, her eyes following something only she could perceive passing.

He asked her if she thought it would be a good thing to be raised on a boat. 'Babies like boats,' she replied. 'A boat's like a cradle, then a doll's house.'

'Do you think you'll be able to live on a boat forever?'

Burgess laughed. 'What's forever, Harry? How long is that?'

'Bricks and mortar can't sink.'

'They can't move either. When I've completed the boat I'll untie the mooring here and go upstream. There are two thousand miles of navigable waterways in this country. You're welcome to come. In three weeks we could be in Yorkshire with a ready-made home. You can see the countryside on a boat from a slow, quiet viewpoint.'

The baby started wriggling between Burgess's thighs, nudging her vagina with her head. 'All this talk of moving and she's trying to get back in,' Harry said. 'Forgot something.'

'Yeah, her manners,' Burgess laughed.

'I can't see myself living on this boat for long, Burgess. It feels like a toy, like something you should grow out of.'

'Neh! That's 'cause you haven't got your shit together yet. The day you left the coast you lost your sense of direction.'

'I couldn't stand that place. It was killing me.'

'Not the sea, Harry. Water won't kill you. The further you stray from water the more evil the world gets. Gravity is original sin.'

He produced a roll of notes from his pocket. He licked his forefinger and thumb and peeled off a hundred pounds. 'I don't want the money, Harry,' she said.

'You should keep it here for the baby. For emergencies. Everyone needs money, Burgess, despite what you say. The days when you could want nothing are over. I'll leave it here.' Harry dumped the money on a table top. They both watched the roll unfurl. 'Do me a favour and take it. Buy yourself a fridge.'

'You don't understand, do you? It would make me feel bad to take the money because it came out of some poor woman's purse. Someone's loss would be my gain and I would feel bad about spending it. It would be wrong.'

'I don't believe what I'm fucking hearing.'

'What *do* you believe in?'

'Myself. Money.'

Burgess reached for his arm and squeezed it. 'I'm very worried that something awful is going to happen to you, Harry. Listen to me. Only when we return to water can there be redemption.'

'You crazy bitch.'

'What is life without water, Harry? ... A desert.'

'Look at this tub ... It's a floating slum.'

'Why not help me then? Keep your money but help me fit out the boat. Pay your rent in labour.'

THREE

The Vaudeville theatre was one of those famous buildings in London that lay outside Harry's sphere of interest. Although he had passed by numerous times its charm had failed to capture him. The awning lights flashed rudely in his face. He stepped into the foyer as a matinée audience was milling around during the interval, clicking their heels, clicking their tongues. Carrying a light raincoat over his arm, Harry started looking for openings: open jackets, open bags. Before any opportunities presented themselves, a bell started ringing. Paranoid by nature, he seized completely, thinking it had something to do with him. The bell was not a warning however, but a call to return to the auditorium. The second half of the play was about to begin. Harry casually drifted in with the crowd and took a seat in the stalls. The house was half full.

When the lights faded several actors appeared on stage in the darkness. Harry leaned forward in his seat as the stage lit up. The play had a rural background, set some time in the past. Men were returning from their labour in the fields, languid and stupid. It depicted the kind of world he had escaped from not so many years ago. He recognized the protagonist from her Equity card photograph in the purse he'd stolen. Gabrielle Scott was one of *his* punters. And he was £400 richer on account of her. In the play she was missing something else as far as he could gather: a progeny. She was a childless wife, shunned by a society in which infertility was deemed tragic, an act of God even. The husband was maudlin and blamed her. As she thrashed around the countryside in a state of bored despair, a virile artisan from the city arrived. This metropolitan stranger was not as he seemed. He had come to hide in the country from crimes committed in the city. He seduces the childless woman in her husband's field.

As these two actors embraced, her nose began to bleed. Two crimson rivers ran down each side of her mouth and dripped off her chin. The realization spread through the audience in a shiver of embarrassment. Gabrielle Scott surfaced through her stage persona, turned to the audience and said in a grey tone, 'I'm sorry but I'll have to go off.'

Pinching her nose, she led the other actors into the wings. Stage lights faded out, house lights faded in. Harry felt the light shining on him. It really was bad luck for her. How often could this happen? He sat it out for another five minutes before the cast returned.

The house lights went out and the stage was lit again. They replayed the same scene, taking it back a few pages in the text. But the audience was restless. They could no longer suspend disbelief. They had come to know that actress personally, while Harry had the jump on them: he had her purse with all its contents.

She becomes pregnant with the stranger's child. To save her husband's honour she shoots herself in the head with a pistol.

The pistol dropped from her hand and she spiralled to the floor. It was a gesture, more than real acting, since no one believed her any longer. She even kept her eyes open when she was supposed to be dead and Harry could have sworn she winked at him. This was the first time he'd been to a theatre in his life, ostensibly to tap a fresh vein of work. Simultaneously, an actor's drills were going to hell. Blood had been spilt. Harry vainly sensed his presence had influenced these changes in routine, as though chance was rooting for them to meet.

FOUR

Charismatic evangelists were pulling huge crowds in Leicester Square. People gathered around to watch the open-air baptisms. Individuals tearfully offered themselves for initiation, stepping up to the large black PVC bathtub, where they were lowered backwards, fully clothed, into the cold water. Charismatics were praying and healing, their hands hovering over the sopping auras of new recruits. Some were talking in tongues, others weeping. A black man with a shaved head held a ten-foot white cross over his shoulder and shouted into a microphone. 'So you own a house, a couple of cars, a stereo, a satellite dish. You got plenty of money to splash around. You think this decade's been good to you. Then I have bad news for you all. That is fool's gold you've been chasing. We have all been short-changed these past years. It has left a god-sized hole in our lives. The bank of the Lord Jesus is the only bank that pays *real* interest, the interest called everlasting life.'

Deep in the heart of things, poaching off the preacher's crowd, Harry was executing his well-rehearsed moves, flicking open catches, plunging and smothering his manoeuvres with mini-collisions against punters, raising his hand up through debris and leather, teasing out joeys. He did not even need to look what he was doing. He was driving blind, huddled by human weight which was hypnotized by Christian-speak and the spectacle of so many people taking cold baths in their clothes.

'There is going to be a revival in this land this present day. There is going to be nothing like it since Adam of old. God is going to give the devil a run for his money. Every animal and living thing is going to hear. Join us now. Hear the music of restoration coming. It'll restore all that politics and lunatics have eaten up. I believe the animal kingdom, the human kingdom, every bit of the kingdom, is going to be restored these last days. Come share our joy. We are the lively ones. We are the glittering stones ...'

Harry found enough work in that one crowd for an hour. It was constantly being renewed with fresh faces and virgin bags hanging on relaxed shoulders. He couldn't get enough of it. Opportunity was lavish. He banqueted, he gorged himself, dipping with the ease of one who can charm the birds out of the trees.

He was still a little high from the morning's heavy quarrying an hour later, walking along the canal tow-path. He hoped to find his fence holed up in the public toilets at Maida Vale, to unload the myriad credit cards he had taken. But the toilets where Denis O'Sullivan worked were locked and Denis gone.

Burgess was on the boat inside the shower unit, building a plinth to raise the new toilet. While Harry had been out stealing in Leicester Square she had adapted a car extractor fan from a breakers' yard, fixing it into the plywood wall and venting it out through a small stainless steel louvre near the gunwale. She was wearing baseball boots, her bare legs fuzzy with hair disappearing up under the hem of her black skirt. She wore a threadbare donkey coat and baby Simmy was strapped to her back with a shawl. Harry carefully hung up his suit and in his underwear he helped fit the toilet, donated to Burgess by another boater.

It was a sea toilet system that would draw water for flushing from the canal. An inlet gate valve had to be fitted below the water-line, so they tilted the boat over to one side by shifting the ballast. Harry lowered himself off the side of the boat into the water and felt like one of those evangelists. Burgess handed him the drill. Up to his waist in water, he cut the hole with the steel-piercing drill, drawing a power line through the latticed ceiling, stealing the electricity from the site. He made a second hole to vent the holding tank near the gunwale, so if the tank were to overfill it would not leak into the bilges. All the pipework was flexible reinforced hose, courtesy of the developers overhead.

Burgess made vegetable stew on a camping stove to keep them going, without bothering to clean the mud off the potatoes before tossing them into the pan. He held the baby as Burgess cooked. Her tiny hands and feet were engrained with dirt and her hair was matted with dust. She looked pale from life underground, away from any sun. Harry had seen Simmy every day now for several months, had got used to her music. He liked the kid well enough, but wanted to keep a distance. The moment her warmth began having a corrosive effect on his defences, Harry always handed her over to Burgess.

After Simmy had drunk deep, she fell asleep at her mother's nipple. Burgess slowly and gently placed the baby on her back on the mattress. She retrieved one hand and as she tried to retrieve the other, the baby prised wide her eyes and cried. Burgess put her back on the breast, where she fell asleep again within seconds. Again she attempted to lay her down, only to fail in the same way. Watching this performance frayed Harry's nerves. He didn't have that patience, didn't want that patience. Tolerance of such a hue and cry was a form of weakness. He could feel anxiety rising up against him and suddenly all he wanted to do was get back on the streets, in among the money, where he could feel strong again.

Harry crossed the river from Waterloo on Hungerford Bridge, running the gauntlet with other people between sombre teenagers squatting on cardboard with mongrel pups. The river was hauling vessels down on an ebb tide. Harry could not relate to the Thames like he could to the canal. It was conspicuously precious, touting confectionery architecture; too obvious, too public. Carrying a small bag from Micky's Boxing Supplies, Harry kept his eyes off the water and off the beggars' faces, single-minded about his mission. Today he was going to meet a famous actress. The motive didn't need much analysis. Every successful man should set himself quests from time to time that have nothing to do with his usual business.

It was a hot May afternoon and the Strand was active with tourists climbing in and out of every doorway, stopping to open street maps. There were more tourists in London than Londoners, if the range of foreign currency Harry was taking was anything to go by. He weaved through the tourists outside the foyer of the Vaudeville theatre, where Gabrielle Scott filled a six-foot poster with her off-centred beauty.

Harry walked around the wall of the building until he found the stage door, then swiftly marched in. His progression was immediately thwarted by a security guard. 'Have you a pass?'

'No ...' Harry saw his plan fall away from him like a stone off a bridge. A receptionist sat behind a bank of telephones. 'I've come to see ...' – he had forgotten the actress's name – 'the one with the nosebleeds. I've been sent over with the medicines.'

The receptionist glared at Harry over her half-rimmed spectacles. Harry showed her the contents of the brown paper bag he was carrying. She looked into the bag and responded positively to the word STERILE on the pack of gauze. 'I'll tell her you're here.'

She tapped out a number. A moment later the security guard was escorting him into the catacombs of the theatre. Harry's eyes darted and lunged. The place was clean and busy, with men and women dressed like American attorneys sliding around the white corridors. The security guard knocked on a door, opening it wide when someone called to enter.

Harry walked into a women's communal dressing-room. Sitting in a chair, Gabrielle Scott addressed his reflection in the mirror. 'You're my medic, I gather?' she said hoarsely. She had just finished a matinée and was still under heavy make-up.

Harry opened his mouth but was too overwhelmed to speak. Near a thousand people had just paid up to £20 to see her. Harry felt he was stealing something here and averted his eyes. He dug his hand into the paper bag and placed the sterilized gauze and bottle of 1–1000 adrenalin on her dressing-table. 'Put some dry gauze up each nostril before you go on stage,' he managed. The other actresses were all in various stages of undress. He knew what a boxers' locker-room looked like and it was nothing like this, even if Gabrielle Scott did resemble a reformed pugilist. Her nose was slightly out of joint, her forehead knuckled and intense.

The security guard leaned nonchalantly against the door-frame. He had been there before, seen too many actresses. 'If you feel a nosebleed coming on,' Harry continued with growing confidence, 'the gauze will stem the flow until you can get off the stage. Have you got a corner somewhere?'

'The wings, you mean?'

'Keep some strips of gauze there and the adrenalin. If you get a nosebleed, soak the gauze in adrenalin and plug your nostrils. It will clot the blood. And that's all you can do, really.'

'Some day I'll get this hooter cauterized. Who sent you over here?'

Harry struggled for a moment. 'I'm a big fan of yours.'

'Well, that's nice.' She picked up the telephone to reserve Harry a seat for the evening performance. Harry didn't care to see the same play again, never wishing to see anything twice. But she ran such an approving smile down his body, Harry changed a lifetime's habit.

'You want to come out and have a drink or something afterwards?'

'All right,' she said.

Harry felt he should say something else now, like, 'Are you sure? Do you know who I am?' It had been so easy he couldn't quite believe it. The famous were so approachable. He now wished he had done this years ago. He caught a glimpse of himself in her mirror as he was backing out, astonished by the image. He had never looked so handsome.

Harry sauntered to the front of house to collect his complimentary, feeling the buzz of achievement. How many men could boast of walking into a theatre for the second time in their life and securing a date with the lead actress? A beautiful actress. Harry was on a roll. He began to scheme a way to take her with him at the end of the night, like a copious joey. Now *that* was rank ambition. Harry puffed out his chest. He was not a man to keep within parameters, to stay with what you were given. You see something you want, you find a way to it. No sooner the word than the deed.

Harry preserved his omnipotence as long as he could in the third row from the front. Every seat in the theatre tonight had a bum on it. Curtain was due up in five minutes. Harry put his head back, closed his eyes and fell asleep.

He sat upright when he felt a pressure against his legs. He opened his eyes to see a tall woman in pink jeans trying to stop herself from falling on him. The rest of the audience were also standing up. 'What's happening?' he asked the woman in pink jeans.

'It's the interval.'

'The interval?' Harry leapt to his feet to let the woman pass.

During the break Harry took his whisky and Perrier to the back of the bar and eavesdropped on the accolades for Gabrielle Scott. Then his interest was diverted to a young couple standing near by: a weak-chinned Caucasian with a careless girlfriend. She had left her leather bag hanging open at the shoulder. Harry walked over to the bar to deposit his empty glass, then swung round, swapping his programme from left to right hand. He dipped his hand into her open bag, masking the action with the programme. He got straight on to what he wanted, pearling it behind the programme, then began the long walk to the toilet with a determined military gait. In a cubicle he opened the joey, rolled his shirt cuffs around the credit cards and wedged the cash – around £80 – into his back trouser pocket. The gutted purse went into the cistern and Harry rejoined the patrons.

In the second half of the play he watched key moments repeat themselves faithfully: Gabrielle Scott's thin calf muscles bulging as she went on tip-toe to bite the sterile husband on the face; the bang of the gun when she shoots herself in the head.

Her voice was like a dredger, singing, screaming, crying. When Harry went to work he made not a sound. Nor did he encourage an audience. He decided there was something wonderful about an actor's liberation, a liberation impossible anywhere but in an imaginary world.

And she went the distance without a nosebleed.

At the end of the play Harry rose to his feet with the rest of the audience to give her an ovation. Her fellow players tactfully withdrew into the wings as a stage-hand presented her with a bouquet of roses. She drew them to her face and pricked her skin on the thorns.

It took five minutes to clear the theatre and find the street, where he ran into Gabrielle Scott outside the stage door. She smiled at him in a generalized way, as if she had forgotten who he was. Harry stood his ground in a crowd thronging to catch a glimpse of her. 'No nosebleed the second time round then?'

Her smile instantly focused. 'My second!' She linked

her arm into his, sweeping him along with her momentum. He may have engineered this encounter, but she was now taking it away from him in the direction of her choice. He gave in to her like a blind man. She still had stage make-up on her face which, for some reason he didn't understand, added to his thrill.

Gabrielle pushed a way through the crowds, who were managing to say with thin breath: 'You were wonderful Miss Scott' and 'Thank you ... I just wanted to say that ... thank you.' Harry could feel a charge from her body as though she'd stored up the tributes like voltage. He felt a little of this victory rub off on him, felt himself grow in stature on her arm.

'Your trick worked,' she began saying as they drew away from the light of the Strand into the darkness of an alley. Gabrielle plucked a piece of bloody gauze from her nostril and flicked it into the gutter. 'I'm starved,' she said. 'Acting's such a *workout*! Let's go get a very quick dinner. Then, Christ! I must go home and *sleep*.'

Harry followed her through a door, walking in her shadow between tables lit by candles. She absorbed the smiles on diners' faces, keeping the secret in her own eyes hidden until she found the table she wanted down at the far end, where she sat with her back to the room.

Harry was flattered to be the sole object of her attention, but it didn't last. Her eyes began to dart around, concentrating only fleetingly on any one thing before passing on. It gave Harry an opportunity to watch her. She had atmosphere, like a tango dancer.

After entertaining others for three hours she seemed to want someone else to perform for her. It felt incumbent on Harry to entertain but he couldn't think what to say. He knew nothing about the theatre. He did not want to talk about himself. Harry lowered his head. 'I must be a let-down after all those people,' he said feebly, beginning to feel he'd won this night out with an actress in a competition.

'I don't want my ego stuck up in the flies like a canary. I need to be brought down.'

'Why is that then?'

'Actors aren't very special, really. Only the text should be revered.' She tugged her hair out of a slide and shook it loose.

Her terms of reference about plays and players so mystified Harry he couldn't raise a single word in reply. In the many silences she twisted her necklace around in her fingers, sucking the fresh-water pearls, and stared blankly at the menu. Her eyes were different colours. One was blue, the other green. Every few minutes she would make new elliptical remarks. 'Actors are their own instruments' was one. 'We are nothing until played', another. Her voice was scandalously deep. She whistled her soft consonants through the gap in her front teeth. He wondered how it would be to drink champagne from her mouth.

Harry felt his way to her heart with flattery. 'If the first time I'd seen you I didn't know you were an actress, I think I'd still know you were, you know, someone special.'

'Wow!' she yawned.

'You have atmosphere, like a tango dancer.' He wished he could walk into a room of strangers and cause a flurry of excitement like she had.

The waiter came to the table and Gabrielle ordered for them both without referring to the menu. She switched the subject to the play. It had been a lost work, hitherto unperformed until the current production. What did he think of childless women?

'I've never really thought about it.'

'Do you have children?' she asked without betraying a flicker of personal interest.

'I'm not married.'

She laughed. 'How nice to meet a conventional man once in a while.'

Dinner came quickly, but not quickly enough for her, it seemed. She ploughed through the first course, rolling fat pancakes of crispy duck and celery. She seemed eager to be away to join what he imagined was far more interesting company elsewhere. There was nothing he could say to slow her down.

'What do you do?' she asked.

Harry always dreaded that question. It was a cheap trick designed to part a man from information to be used against him. 'I do everything,' he replied, 'from A to Z.'

'Achilles Heels repairs to Zebra painting,' she returned instantly.

'Along those lines.'

'No, really, tell me ... What do you do under G and B. For Great Britain.'

'Grin and bear it.'

'Ah! Hahaha! Very good. Are you an actor? Haven't I seen you in something?'

'Not an actor.' Harry's reply seemed to wither her. Gabrielle gave off an air of insecurity, like a child who had wet the bed. Harry did not realize that actors preferred their own kind. They do not care much for civilians. In real terms, Gabrielle Scott's life-experience was far more limited than most people's. She lived constantly with a slow-burning fear of being found out. Acting entails more dishonesty than honesty: the dishonesty of pretending to be someone else. Without either one realizing, Harry and Gabrielle had stumbled across their natural ally in life.

Harry knew that people are all the more powerful for not answering questions. He held out until Gabrielle stopped tracking him and began regaling him instead with pointless epics about show business in a quick and silvered tongue. Her voice was like an adjutant to her own self. A colourful other character. While Harry had plenty of work stories of far greater interest, he couldn't trade on them socially. He began to feel edged out.

Harry was impatient to be off. This relationship was already on the rocks. He had proved the wherewithal to get an actress around the table but now it was time to leave before victory turned cold.

A leather jacket hung from the back of a chair at the next table. Excusing himself, he made for the gents, taking a pig-skin wallet out of the jacket on the way. Behind a locked door in the toilets he rifled through the contents, feeling a surge of superiority as he yanked out a wedge of twenties.

When Harry returned, the bill was brought on a plate. Gabrielle reached for it but Harry got there first and left £100 to settle a £68 tab to show her the kind of money he was worth.

There was a shadow beyond their table and Gabrielle leaned her chair into it. Harry went looking for her face in the darkness. Her mouth dropped open into a small laugh, laced with a little terror. She let her chair crash forward and he saw her face was wide open with exigencies. 'I just saw you steal a wallet from that man's jacket.'

Harry looked for the door, gauging the distance. There were no obstacles in the way. With five bounds he could be out. Gabrielle arrested him with her hand on his sleeve and squeezed his wrist. He looked at her again and saw something he had never seen on a woman's face: a look of enchantment for what she had seen him do. He saw all the possibilities he had dreamed about happening between them, widening in her green and blue eyes. He had just done something skilful and *disreputable*, and it had been done in real life. Harry didn't know it yet, but he was someone she could use for material.

His theft had moved them along. Harry felt a breeze come through an open window. She looked away briefly, her eyes flaring with private thought. She zoomed in on him again. 'How did you steal that wallet? You had it out as though you had a magnet in your hand.'

'That's for me to know and you to find out.'

'Can you steal a watch?' She was getting higher all the time. He was beginning to thrill her.

'No one steals watches any more, unless you work in a circus.'

'What kind of pickpocket are you? Are you violent?'

'Steamers are the violent ones. The smother game's my game.'

'What's that?'

'An art from the past. It's been pushed aside by more violent methods, steaming. But I work like a mosquito. Out of reach by the time the bite starts itching.'

'How do you do it? How would you steal my purse?'

'How did you learn to act?'

'It took me years.'

'Do you think my business came about overnight?'

'Have you ever been to prison?'

'Briefly.'

Harry and Gabrielle talked incessantly now. Their questions and answers kept on running and bubbling. A constant flow of people were passing the table on any kind of pretext to look at Gabrielle Scott, blinking hard as if her light was too bright for their eyes. They looked Harry over too, beaming hostility at him for being nobody in a designer suit.

Maybe all he had was his suit, but at least he'd enchanted Gabrielle Scott by paying the dinner bill with stolen revenue. He always knew that one day money would buy him charisma. Money was improving a whole lot of people's self-esteem. Money was a benign force, including stolen money.

Outside the restaurant Gabrielle said, 'Come back home and I'll give you a nightcap, since you ended up paying for the meal. We can get a cab there.'

With a subtle flick of her wrist Gabrielle brought a taxi slithering to her feet in the Strand.

She owned a large flat in an Edwardian mansion in North Kensington. Harry figured he could fit Burgess's boat neatly into her hall, which was sprinkled with pink light from a rose petal lamp. Sparse furnishings in an adjoining room were silhouetted in the spill of the same light. Harry expected to be shown in there as soon as she had retrieved her key from the door. She tossed it into a Mexican ceramic bowl brimming with duplicate keys. Harry never got to see the living-room. Gabrielle pulled him by the hand into a darkened bedroom. A street light shone through the curtainless window and oranged the bed. 'Come and get your nightcap,' she said in a German kommandant's accent and he got to drink champagne after all.

They kissed for a long time, her tongue busy and explorative. He let her pull him on the bed, her hair replacing her tongue in his mouth. She yanked at his belt, and he hauled her skirt over her athletic thighs. In the dark he put his hand around a deep contour and discovered bare flesh leading into moist underwear. She was wearing stockings and suspender belt. He struggled to make the right response, the street light flooding the room highlighting his awkwardness. He decided not to tamper with the apparatus and made a quick and clumsy entry.

In the next moment he was pumping out a rich hot sap, rolling off her, wondering where he had left his jacket with his money. He thought it might be in the hall. He didn't like being where he couldn't see it.

Gabrielle sat up in the dark and lit a cigarette. 'I'm pregnant, Harry.'

'It takes a little longer than that, I think.'

'I took a test from the chemist today and it came out positive. Of course, it could be wrong. But I don't think so.'

'Who's the father?'

'I don't know.'

'You must know.'

'I can narrow it down to two, I suppose.'

'What are you going to do?'

'I don't know that either. I don't want to have an abortion. But there's another complication. My boy-friend has been in prison the last twelve months.'

'He's a screw ...' This seemed the only possibility to Harry.

'An inmate, on judge's remand.'

'So he's not the father then?'

'That much I do know.'

'You seem to like thieves, don't you?' He was disappointed. 'I thought I'd be your first one.'

'Actors and thieves are temperamentally very similar.'

'I guess so.'

'Do you realize this is the third time today I've had sex with a thief? Twice on stage and you, for real. He's trying to get bail pending an appeal, Harry.'

'Your boyfriend?'

'If he finds me knocked up, I don't know what he'll do.'

'Is he violent?'

'Potentially. Maybe. There is another thing. I'm ashamed to admit this ... Well ... you're going to think this is pathetic, but I was supposed to play Portia in a few months' time.'

'Who is Portia?'

'I've got a new handle on her, you see. Portia is normally played as a spoilt girl, very smug, believes money can solve all problems. Anti-Semitic. But that's production, not text. Suitors offer her money and she rejects them. Why would she do that if all she cared for was money? I think she's a Rapunzel waiting to be released from the boredom of Belmont. The merchants fight over money and she teaches them compassion. In five months' time we were due to start rehearsing.'

She began to sob with her body pressed against the cold grey plaster of the wall. Although the nuances of her problem escaped Harry, seeing this great actress, this important person, in tears inspired him to want to do kind deeds. He tried to find her face in the dark with his hands and sensed her mouth all wet. He turned her over and smelled blood. Her arms locked around him like a frightened child and her voice squirrelled up an octave in the darkness. 'Don't leave me tonight.'

No one had done or given him anything in his life and he had always coped well with that. He preferred it with no debts to pay. But now his ancient defence was crumbling at the edges. Harry didn't feel he had the authority to contradict her. However irrational it might be, he felt responsible for her well-being.

He petted her hair and tried to think again if he really wanted to be in this position. He couldn't see her face any more. She could have been anyone now. All people are equal in the dark. Fame is nothing without light. Then he told himself to have a little foresight. If it all proved a big mistake, taking orders from her, he was sure to find something worth stealing in the flat. He felt so comforted by his wisdom that it put him to sleep.

In his dream that night Harry was locked in a cell, watching a black Daimler pulling into the prison court-yard. It parked outside the hospital and an obese person was barrelled out of the swing-doors. He was so fat his arms and legs had sunk into his body. Two prison officers, failing to lift him through the car door, began shoulder barging and kicking him. The Daimler was flying an official flag on the bonnet and drove off with the man wedged in the doorway, his feet scraping along on the ground.

Harry woke distressed. It was always the same. Whenever he dreamed he recalled something he'd actually seen happen. Dreams were meant to be an escape from reality.

He wondered if this was some kind of punishment. Harry's greatest unarticulated fear was reaching a final day of reckoning, when all the people he'd cheated on would gang up on him in his dreams. For the remains of the night he perched on the rim of sleep beside the actress, waiting for light to break.

FIVE

Harry listened in earnest to Gabrielle's descriptions of her boyfriend, Peter Samson, and tried to learn something about what women want. Whenever she visited the prison, he came out of the hatch into the visitors' room with his hair combed, moustache trimmed, freshly shaved, and talked about business. Harry knew that in a society of men without women it was all too easy to become physically degenerate, to let conversation slip into pornography. So Harry was impressed with the image of this man smelling of cologne, while others reeked of stale tobacco and sweat.

He regretted never having met a criminal as exotic as Peter Samson. As explained by Gabrielle, while they drank peach champagne in her garden, Samson was a property developer who specialized in real estate around water. A Welsh castle on the Severn estuary was now his polo club. A gothic miners' rest home on a Scottish loch had found new riparian tenants who flew up on weekends for the fishing. He converted warehouses and filled empty spaces with bricks and mortar for bright young people who could afford a view of river or sea.

His company had offices in London and Munich. Some unlawful deal was financed in Britain through his Munich office. For the year he'd spent on judge's remand he had been litigating to be tried in Germany. In London, one of his colleagues had been sentenced to three-to-five for property-related crimes. In Germany the going rate was a fine for the same thing. But the English court dismissed his habeas corpus argument. Now he was appealing to the House of Lords, hoping to be bailed out, pending that appeal.

And that was all she knew. Samson would not talk about the details of his offence. Harry, who remembered only too well how most inmates liked to talk of nothing else, believed every word Samson never said.

Harry thought about Samson a good deal more while lying in Samson's half of her bed. He owned a seven-bedroom apartment in Mayfair, a mansion in Sussex, a château outside Munich, an £80,000 car and a helicopter. He earned a six-figure salary legitimately, so why did he need to steal anything?

'To keep the women coming, that is why. *Coming* in the sexual sense.' Harry didn't understand what Gabrielle meant. She talked of someone called the New Age woman, who had become so masculine, such a *conqueror*, she had changed the aspirations of men, forcing them to extend their horizons, often beyond the law, just to stay in the game. Ruthless power, violent success: these were the modern aphrodisiacs.

Harry broke out in a sweat hearing this. He wondered if he could ever stay the pace.

'He did it all without leaving the room, Harry.' Gabrielle was still impressed. Her glass ran over with peach champagne. 'That's the new way of doing crime. Being streetwise, like you, uh ... well. That's just loose change, isn't it?'

Harry brooded severely. He felt she had put him down. He knew he'd have to improve his grid position if he was to keep up with Samson. Keep her coming.

After the habeas corpus hearing failed, Samson tried to go over the wall. But he didn't make it and was stripped of association time and company. Visiting orders were suspended and Gabrielle last saw him several months ago. Harry pictured his solitary figure walking the circle alone in the exercise yard, wearing the E-man yellow stripe down the leg of his trousers, head bowed, ashamed to have betrayed the actual level of his despair.

The week before Harry entered her life, Gabrielle received a letter from Samson, saying he was optimistic about getting bail. 'That's why I'm so edgy. I said I'd be faithful to him. I did stay on the wagon too, for about six months. Then I weakened. A couple of times. Now I'm in the club.' She quietly began to cry again.

She was dressed in striped T-shirt, faded black dungarees and a sweat-band keeping her hair out of her face, which was plain and pale without make-up. Harry tried to imagine her alongside the kind of wolfish, sassy women who came on visiting orders to prison, dressed in furs and with long bare legs crossed below the table. The more exotic the criminal the more attractive the woman on his VO. Gabrielle broke this rule; she must have looked very unexceptional. No man would look twice if he didn't know who she was. But this was the point: Samson knew who she was. As *the* exotic criminal he wanted beauty of a more enduring kind. Men who knew who she was looked up to Gabrielle and from that angle she was the fairest of them all.

But what did she want from Harry? He had no special gifts. She liked the idea of him being a thief, but how long would that last? As long as her play lasted? Was it just an infatuation? He did seem to comfort her in pregnancy, listened to her talk away her apprehensions. But if it was just comfort she wanted, she could have chosen from any number of people. In the last three weeks Harry estimated that eight thousand had seen her on stage. Eight thousand people had all paid to see her. So why did she encourage Harry, for whom an audience of one was a prelude to disaster? But maybe that was it. They say opposites attract.

To Harry it was a revelation finding a kindred spirit in the world. Even though acting was not a crime, there was something dishonourable about it. It was also a very elusive profession and getting to spend time with her was not a simple matter. He snatched an hour here and there before she was away with other people in another part of the country. It was a piecemeal love-affair, if it was a love-affair at all. The way she operated there was no chance of her becoming a regular kind of spouse. They'd meet for breakfast at 2 pm and lunch at 7 pm. She was habitually late by between one and three hours. The record was five. When she finally turned up that night the first thing she said she had to do was make a telephone call. At a kiosk outside their rendezvous she made a rash of calls on her phonecard, while Harry waited inside. After an hour Harry lost patience and went out to the kiosk to find her asleep, leaning against the telephone with the receiver against her face like a baby's dummy.

It was impossible to say where her day began and where it ended, where their relationship began or whether they had one at all. For a week in June she made three television commercials ('for the ackers') as well as five shows of the Lope de Vega play. All week she was getting 4 am calls, wrapping at 6 pm and going straight to the theatre from the set. Even then she could not bear to miss a party. She survived on catnaps, looking ghosted most of the time. One Sunday they went swimming together and she fell asleep in the crowded pool.

It bothered him that she fell asleep on their dates. 'Why don't you just spend a night in, once in a while? Sleep all day Sunday.'

'I'm too wired to sleep, Harry. I only drop off if I haven't planned to.'

One afternoon she fell asleep in the middle of sex. Harry lay with her head gently snoring on his chest for hours. It was their longest date yet. He left her sleeping because he didn't want her to wake and find him there, as if he had nothing better to do than watch her sleep.

As he was letting himself out he stole a set of spare keys to her flat from the Mexican bowl near the door. There were six or seven sets of the keys, so he doubted if she'd miss one lot. She had more important things going on in her life than to count her spare keys with every entrance and exit.

During one fortnight in which she was too busy to see him at all, Harry went alone to all the matinée performances of the de Vega play, slipping in for free during the intervals. He had yet to see the first half. To the thief from Madrid with whom her character has the affair, Gabrielle had begun responding quite differently. Since knowing Harry she had intensified her feeling towards the Spaniard, made him all the more interesting and sexy by virtue of her fervour. The performances now began to burn.

The play was the only time he saw her behave to a

pattern. When she acted, she told him, she liked to keep a secret from the audience, a little dark spot on her psyche perforating her character. Usually this entailed using some psychotic emotion previously unexplored. It helped her to frighten people. In the de Vega her secret was pregnancy. She played the barren wife with a real personality growing inside her. This was one secret to which Harry was privy. He went to see the play so many times to feel an advantage over her audiences.

After his last visit to the theatre he put his body in front of the stage door. She bowled out and into him. Gabrielle hooked her arm into his. 'I've got to meet some people, Harry,' she apologized. 'Share the taxi with me there. We can have that time together.'

Harry didn't see any reason why he couldn't go with her to meet these people. She responded negatively. 'I need my space, Harry.'

Space as far as he knew it was an empty arena, not a constellation of other people. However she became a possessive woman for the fifteen minutes of taxi ride and drew him out of his abject mood. 'Do you have any secrets from me, Harry? Are you married, for instance?'

'Don't be ridiculous.'

'How would I know? You go off, I don't know where to. But sometimes I wonder.' Gabrielle had been too self-absorbed to ask such questions of him till now. It had to be the pregnancy. Pregnancy made women insecure. A woman enamoured of the moment who is suddenly chained to an uncharted future would query what her companion did in his absence. That Harry was not the father seemed a trivial technicality, since she didn't know who the father was, anyway. 'You tell me so little about your life, Harry.'

'What do I know of yours? You lead several lives.' Harry didn't believe that for a moment. If he was being inscrutable it was to cover a dull life; a basic existence on the canal with a melancholy wretch and her baby. He too lived in fear of being found out.

He was flattered by her curiosity, even though he began to suspect it was an act. But he was a fraud himself, knew the rules and liked the game. Good thieves, good actors were susceptible to their own lies, could change something fake into something true, or something true into something else.

In Islington he watched her walk away from the taxi, up the steps to a house and longed to be with her. Everything she touched turned to gold. She was so perfect. She never had a dull moment. But she wasn't his. He never felt once that she belonged to him.

The taxi took Harry to the canal at Marylebone. He persuaded the driver to have a drink with him in a pub. Having a drink with Gabrielle's driver was as close as he could get to her.

SIX

Equipped with his own key, Harry habitually let himself into Gabrielle's apartment whenever he judged she'd be out somewhere. He strolled through the rooms, feeling her strong presence in the air, the bed sheets, in the bathroom. He'd take a shower with her body oils, then stalk around in a towel smelling of sandalwood and camphor, eating anything he could find in the fridge. He didn't really care if he left personal traces. It would do her no harm to be reminded of him, to know Harry Langland had been in the neighbourhood.

Early one morning when Gabrielle was at a radio studio in Bristol, Harry padded around her kitchen with a cup of black coffee. He looked out of the window into the garden, uncertain of where he should start work. Jimmy had made those decisions for him. Sometimes he missed the company, missed the wiseguys cracking all their jokes after sorties on punters in rainbow plaid. He also missed making their kind of money. But what you lost on the roundabouts you gained on the swings. He didn't have Victor around, compromising him with violence. Harry felt a lot safer, that was for sure.

The activity in the communal garden distracted him. It was busy with people walking small dogs, scooping up their crap in shovels, and nannies pushing their charges on a tree swing. If Gabrielle came in through the front door right now Harry could get out of the flat by the back door. He had all the keys, including those for the two wrought-iron gates at each end of the garden that led to the street and directly out to Regent's Canal.

He tossed his coffee dregs into the sink. Five minutes later he was leaving the flat via the garden, with a bundle of toilet tissue in his pockets and a light raincoat over his arm. The garden was such a paradise he wanted it to go on forever. It was full of huge trees and lilac tulips, yellow roses. Pink and white façades of Edwardian houses screened off the city. Providing you could meet the monthly mortgage repayments, this was architecture to rejoice in. The only people left in London still to believe in utopias all lived there, sharing the same view into the laburnums as Gabrielle. He walked with his face tilted upwards at five-storey terraces with decorative balustrades. Hundreds of sash windows reflected the white clouds in the blue sky. He felt like a provincial boy suddenly, in a port, watching big ships. The sensation he got strolling along was of distant places rather than a celebration of wealth. A middle-aged man in a tracksuit jogged past him on the seashell path, making a spectacle of himself. Harry never ran anywhere if he could help it. Running was an act of guilt and it made him uneasy just to watch. The jogger ruined the peace. Harry quickened his pace to the south gate.

Every working environment had its own rhythm. It was Harry's first time in this market and he strolled around for a while, learning the tune. Two German tourists asked him to take their photograph. Starting the day with a benevolent act had brought him good karma in the past. He held their Nikon to his face. In the frame behind the two smiling blonde girls was a policeman ingratiating himself with the stallholders. Harry imprisoned him in celluloid. A group of Africans handed round a few beers on the corner, shuffling their feet, getting a bit of sun, letting others do the toiling. Kids ran in between the stalls banging on car roofs. A bus traversed the lane, ejecting youths as it moved. They looked up into the sky as if for direction, into cracks in the wall, colliding with one another. Watches, mirrors, fish eyes spewed out of black bags pricked by cats and glittered in the morning sun. A security van swept away from the bank with a squeal of tyres. A pregnant woman distributed coffee in polystyrene cups. It was a peaceful day. Tramps nosed around the stalls for windfall fruit. Harry began to catch the tenor of the place.

He leaned up against a jeweller's window as a young black outfit in squeaking leathers and white sneakers cantered up the lane. They were a posse of steamers reconnoitring the market and he wanted to let them get ahead. Steamers knocked their punters down to get the bags off their shoulders. It was a modern art form Harry wished to be dissociated from. He regarded himself as part of a more established institution, like the monarchy. He noted the direction they took and passed a few minutes looking in the window. Immediately below his face was a diamond line bracelet. It was priced at £3,500. Harry decided he had to have it for Gabrielle.

His camouflage was the appearance of ease. He floated rather than walked, searching for punters – such as the young woman in a Laura Ashley dress bending over a jewellery case, her concentration all in her fingertips. Harry came along broadside. He took the weight of her bag in his right hand and gave the clasp a hard flick to open it. With his left hand covered by his mac he felt for some feature, soft leather, bulk of coins. The joey had to come up quickly or he would walk away. Fifty per cent of the time he came out of bags empty-handed and that would be that. The dip had failed. There was no going back into the same bag twice. There was no second take in his business as there was in Gabrielle's. This time he was on the money. He felt a surge of euphoria as he ducked into the porch of a Portuguese delicatessen.

Under the raincoat Harry rifled through the contents of the joey like a photographer developing film in a light-proof bag. He removed the cash and wrapped the joey in toilet paper and hauled back to the street. Flowing with the crowds he wiped his nose with the tissue and pushed the bundle into a pile of rotting fruit.

Women were exclusively his quarry. Taking from them was how he related to them. It let them know of his existence. He liked to think of them returning home and discovering their losses while their husbands were still at work, then blushing at the thought of some anonymous man having frisked them.

He masked his movements well and punters were the last to know what he was doing to them. Only the dip squads knew what to look for. They moved around all the time in an active area, performing the same dance, their heads swinging from side to side like noddy dogs in a car window. He had to try to rumble them before they rumbled him, by their eye movements. Dip squads' eyes did much the same thing, which is to say they surveyed all activity at waist level. That's why he wrapped joeys in tissue paper, for who threw away leather wallets? If he clocked the dip squad clocking him, the only thing to do was get out of the area, right out of the area. In this market where the men hanging around were mainly black, dip squads would stand out like ghosts. This kind of advantage made him nonchalant.

Most thieves are fantasists and you would have to look no further than Harry for evidence. As soon as his fingers knocked on sunken treasure he was off on some voyage in his head. In the shelter of crowds he deified himself, became something money couldn't buy. It was his mind's defence against moral problems and kept his heart from calcifying. But it was a dangerous habit to lay himself open in that way. He often got lost in a fantasy, surfacing with a joey in his hand and no recollection of how it got there.

He wanted to be someone Gabrielle would look up to. She looked up to military advisors, hard news journalists, those who went out and found trouble. Experience is sexy to one who lives in an imaginary world. Harry began to build himself a character as he squeezed between bodies on the lane of antique stalls. In the swollen crowd he developed the idea of being an enigma. Pickpockets were enigmas. Stealthful, invisible, solitary. Being a coastal man, he gave himself a merchant ship to command. But he was more than just a sea captain. Harry Langland was something in the theatre. Specifically, he had written ... *The Merchant of Venice*.

He took shore leave in Gravesend to see his own play premièred, with Gabrielle in the lead role. And it came as a surprise to him, as all great writing should surprise its author, as though someone else had written it. After the performance he stepped out into the blue street and left a note on yellow paper for Gabrielle at the stage door. In her dressing-room she read Harry's signature at the bottom of the note, the ink still damp on the paper. Without a word of explanation to anyone in her dressing-room she threw on mufti and rushed to the stage door, where Harry was looking like the young Marlon Brando. They went to a restaurant across the road and everyone recognized who she was. But tonight she was in awe of Harry Langland, who had created her. Over dinner he made her cry with a story of a nuclear test explosion he'd seen from his ship in the South Pacific and how he had to radio the company for five days' compassionate leave for the crew, who were traumatized by the image of the holocaust they'd seen.

Then something disastrous happened.

A woman swung a carrier bag full of books into Harry's face. A joey spilled out of his hand. He was knocked off his feet. A hurricane filled his ears. Stall-holders were staring, she was shouting, and if she hadn't been Portuguese it could have ended a lot worse for him. Adrenalin pumped him back on his feet, up and running.

When he could run no further he stopped to look over his shoulder. He was in the clear and relaxed his shoulders against a garden wall. Two young kids were begging outside a Doner Kebab. The inner city had become so crowded with homeless, an exodus had begun into the suburbs. They were like sharks, mindless of territory, dumping in your garden, blocking entrances and exits in an erstwhile serenity like Notting Hill. But in Harry's mind they were following him around. He knew it was only his skill as a thief which preserved him from a similar life. But for the moment the zest of charity was in him, like a sea spray, and he dug deep into his pocket for money. He handed one of the boys £20 to dispel the bad karma.

He found a way to the Paddington arm of the Grand Union canal by Carlton Bridge. He went down on his knees and scooped a handful of water to wipe his worried face. The water was churlish and cold. He felt a crab-like security returning as he walked by the water, under the Westway flyover past St Mary Magdalene church and the Warwick housing estate. At a sanitary station he jumped over a hosepipe feeding into a narrow boat. He looked through the portholes at the petite environment inside, half expecting to see dolls sitting in there drinking tea. He left the canal at Delamere Terrace and strolled randomly to the bridge, his head empty of thought. He stopped to lean against the wrought-iron bridge facing Browning's Pool, the point where the Paddington arm meets Regent's Canal. This was the only section of the canal that catered for tourists. The Regency architecture, floating art gallery and restaurant, the classically restored barges, seemed part of the same museum. Cherry trees lining the street were in bloom and their pink blossom floated on the water.

After a moment or two he decided to be off again but was in a contrary state of mind about so many things and couldn't decide which way to go. The tow-path was blocked by private moorings between the bridge and Maida Hill tunnel. Where the roads led seemed arbitrary.

While he was marooned on the bridge, a well-known entrepreneur emerged from one of the houseboats moored in the basin. He left the tow-path for Blomfield Road. Harry snapped back into gear and began to follow him. This man was a heavyweight. He owned an airline, a record company and a large chunk of London. It would often pay to follow such a punter all day if necessary, waiting for the right moment. One of Harry's biggest pay-offs came from trailing a Saudi after seeing him one morning make a huge withdrawal from a bank. Harry followed him shopping, through Hyde Park, to a mosque, ending up in Langan's Brasserie in the evening. The Saudi ordered a well-cooked steak sandwich before going to the gents. As he washed his face in a basin full of water, Harry swept his briefcase off the floor with £4,000 in cash inside.

But Harry would have sacrificed the short-term goal of his wallet to ask the man how he made a stash when, as everyone knew, he didn't have one to begin with. How do men like you and me get a foothold? he wanted to say. But the man suddenly wasn't there any more. He had stepped into a chauffeur-driven Mercedes in the street and sped off in a meaningful direction. Harry wandered listlessly into the Lisson Grove estate to join the tow-path again.

Between two railway bridges Harry recognized his fence, Denis O'Sullivan, lying under a bench outside the public convenience, firing a slingshot at the pigeons. Pigeons were to Denis on the out what nonces were on the inside: vermin that needed culling. Every system has its pecking order. Everyone needs his scapegoat.

When Harry kicked the sole of his shoe, he rolled from under the bench, bristling with pent-up violence. He had tears tattooed below his eyes and a spider's web across his forehead. When he recognized Harry he went off the boil. He came to his feet clutching a plastic bin-liner.

They sat on the bench rolling cigarettes from Denis's

tobacco pouch. Denis rolled his thin as a matchstick as though still rationed to a prison issue of half an ounce a week. When heavy smokers in prison ran out of tobacco they used to tail other smokers in the exercise yard, waiting to dive for the butts. As a squat figure, Denis was that much closer to the ground and usually got to them first. He was always very proud of that. Denis could have been inhaling on a Marlboro now, a Camel filter, even a richer brand of tobacco. He didn't, because it never occurred to him to do so.

'If I kill twenty pigeons a day how long will it take me to make a mark? Do you think I'm flogging a dead horse, Harry? Tell me the truth.'

'If it gives you satisfaction, Denis ...'

'Well, it does. I hate the sight of them on the scrounge all the time. All they ever want to do is eat. They never fly anywhere, or sing.'

Harry laid his head back, eyes closed to the sun and let the smoke pour out of his nostrils. He inhaled another wad of smoke. His shoulders began loosening after all the stress they'd been put under.

The sound of infants sharpened Harry's drifting mind. A class of children were being escorted by their teachers across Prince Albert Road and over the bridge. A length of rope tied around their waists held them together like a chain-gang. Harry found the image of these infant inmates very disconcerting and he tensed up again.

Denis filled his slingshot and took aim at an albino pigeon waddling along the tow-path. But his heart wasn't in it and he missed. 'Which direction did you come from just now, Harry?'

'From Maida Vale.'

'If you'd come the other way you'd have seen the frogmen. They found another leg in the canal.'

'Whose?'

'I don't know *whose* fucking leg it is. But they've got one. And it matches the arm they found here two years ago.'

'How do they know it belongs with the other one?'

'Forensic.'

'Did you kill anyone?'

'I did not. The Old Bill think the boaters might have done someone in.'

'That's stupid.'

'It's the Old Bill. What do you expect?' Denis filled his slingshot with another stone. He pulled back the elastic to his face. Before he could release the stone, the elastic came adrift from the aluminium catapult and slapped him in the eye. 'Fuck! Fucking hell! That hurt like shit! I bought this bloody catapult only the other day. It's probably fucking Japanese.'

A great man once said the English find out who they are in a public toilet. But then he didn't know Denis. Denis was a council lavatory attendant; the gents' toilet outside the park was his territory. He had a private cubicle of his own, ten by fifteen feet, with a table and moulded fibreglass chair, a kettle and a large black and white TV. He sat in this room at intervals during the day and people came to him to buy credit cards and drugs: Visa, Access, American Express; grass, ecstasy, speed and LSD. His principles wouldn't allow him to sell heavy drugs, nor sell to minors. This was typically shortsighted of him. What was the point of trafficking drugs if you had a problem with ethics? If he couldn't sell smack by the kilo then he should have been in something else. Harry had tried telling him this time and again. The way to success, Harry knew, was never to limit your line of business.

Pigeon-slayer, toilet-cleaner, drug-pusher, credit-card fence. You would be hard-pressed to find a man with a lower caste than his. Denis regarded Harry as his best friend and Harry quite liked Denis, but he preferred to limit their transactions to business. Denis was not a social asset to anyone who had dreams of ascendancy.

'Have a look at these cards.' Harry fished out a joey he'd kept from the market and tugged on a cluster of credit cards: Barclay's Visa, Lloyd's Access, Nat West Switch, Esso. 'They're fresh out the sea, Denis. Give me fifty quid each. Or one-seventy-five the lot.'

'All right. But you'll have to come back to the flat. I ain't got no money here.'

There was no more work left in his trembling hands that morning, so Harry went with Denis. On the way out Denis wiped a slab of porcelain with a wet mop and threw a handful of disinfectant cubes into the urinals.

Denis's car was on the street. Looking at it, Harry felt exonerated for not owning one. It was a 1979 fairground attraction with its back end hitched up on jeep tyres. Harry opened the car door. The cockpit was a house of games, covered floor to ceiling in fake fur, with two rally seats, a square steering-wheel and a stuffed pigeon dangling on fishing gut from the rearview mirror.

'You carry drugs in this thing?' Harry asked.

'I shift them around, yeah.' Denis held his black sack over a park dustbin. 'You want any of these birds?'

Harry managed to shake his head and Denis tossed away the bag.

The engine made a very wild noise. The windows were tinted, but not dark enough for Harry, who sank as far as he could into the rally seat.

Denis squatted in a rustic Victorian tenement with a view from his window of the King's Cross gas holders. His housemates were a grab-bag of Irish hitmen, pimps and teenage runaways rotating every few months. Denis had been there the longest, since his release date back in eighty-six. He sprang two padlocks on the reinforced door which opened into a room slightly larger than his toilet cubicle. A single bed covered in a gangrenous yellow sheet was crushed in a corner next to a Baby Belling stove on a tea chest. Dark green polystyrene tiles brought the ceiling down upon their heads. Denis stood on the bed and lifted the corner of a ceiling tile. Gingerly he brought out his nest egg. He counted off £200 and replaced the stash. He jumped off the bed and gave Harry all but £25.

Denis prepared a three-course meal out of cans: tomato soup, beef casserole, peaches and evaporated milk. He warmed the soup on the Baby Belling and talked like an inmate, like someone short on company for too long. 'Have you noticed how the angel on a Rolls-Royce is held onto the bonnet? Aaron McQueen gave me twenty good ones to get a gold-plated one for his roller. They're held on with a fucking *chain*, not a wire, like Aaron said they were. Like a bicycle chain. I broke my hacksaw trying to saw it off. I had to get a new blade from Homebase before I could ...'

'Shut up, Denis.'

Denis ground his story to a halt. He went back to his soup. They were sitting side by side on the bed, resting their soup on their knees. Harry was trying to protect his suit with a tabloid newspaper. Denis gripped his bowl so tightly his knuckles whitened around the words LOVE and DETH tattooed into his fingers. Then he raised the bowl to his lips and his hair caught in the soup. Harry put his soup bowl on the floor and pushed it away with his foot. 'You eat like a fucking con, Denis. I bet you never get invited out to dinner.'

Denis scooped some casserole from the dented saucepan into his empty soup bowl. The casserole looked like dog food. Even prison food looked better, which really was incriminating. The casserole was the last straw. Harry called a rain check on that as well as the dessert and returned to work.

Harry never operated in any one territory more than a couple of hours at a time, nor returned to the same place twice in a week. He let the tide come in and out to clean his footprints off the sand. Golders Green was clean; he hadn't been over there in months. Golders Green was a good target because it was woman country. They drove up the kerbs in Mercedes, parking on double yellow lines, then after concluding some serious purchase, they moved the car on fifty metres to the next boutique. He wondered about the men they had married. Were they New Age men, like Peter Samson? Substantial providers for sure.

The weather had turned humid, which was Harry's kind of day. It made people lethargic and careless. A Tory candidate was canvassing from an open-topped bus on the High Street. The vehicle was painted up like a carnival bus, filled with people in blue paper-hats. 'The police have the full support of the Conservative party,' the candidate was saying through a megaphone – 'Britain is fully respected abroad. Our defence system is once again strong.'

Harry cased a kosher deli affording a good view from outside of any dummies that might be on the floor. There seemed to be quite a few pieces of work lying here and there and so Harry wandered in with a businesslike air. He put a newspaper down to reserve a table, while gesturing to the maître d' that he wanted to use the lavatory before he did anything else. In the restaurant were clusters of European Jews who had something of the Old Country about them. They sounded as though they were singing. Harry allowed himself a moment to listen to their plaintive Yiddish. He liked these people. As a goy he was extraneous to them. They made him feel invisible, which was just the job, made things that much easier. He crossed to a table full of women, inhaling a powerful scent of their lacquered hair as he kicked a dummy along the floor towards the toilet.

There was so much nonsense in the bag it took a while to find the joey. It came to the surface, corpulent and soft like a ripe peach. Eleven credit cards were strung together in plastic. He kept eight of the cards and the cash and tipped the rest into the lavatory cistern. To make his exit seamless he dropped a £1 tip in the cashier's tray on the way out.

Harry crossed the street and took cover in a health club. The moment he arrived he felt like sitting down to drink a freshly squeezed orange juice and eat a piece of the carrot cake being sold at a bar. He always wanted to retire after the first strike. There was always this problem with motivation in being self-employed, but you had to keep the momentum up in his profession as in any other.

The women wandering around in the club were all in their forties and early fifties, but in dim light, in their leotards, they could have passed for twenty-five. They had the bodies of young girls. Harry felt suddenly depressed in there among them, constantly failing in the task they had set themselves: to keep their youth. He took a holdall bag off the back of a seat, concealing it under his jacket. At the exit he delayed his leaving to pick up an aerobics class schedule – a good piece of business Gabrielle might have appreciated.

He had to find a place to lose the pink dummy. He ducked into a hotel and followed the arrows for the toilets into the basement. He examined the contents: towel, dirty underwear, make-up bag, hairbrush with long blonde strands caught in the bristles, a framed photograph of two girls in school uniform. But there was no joey. He'd drawn a cadaver and the dummy went flying into the air. He counted the money from the restaurant to improve his mood. £100, all in £5 notes.

He washed his hands at the sink, dampened his face. It was very hot and the whining extractor fan was ineffectual in dispelling the soporific air. The open door afforded a view of a long silent corridor carpeted in what looked like fallen autumn leaves. Above his head women's pointed heels clicked across the glass skylight. A window in the toilet was reinforced with wire and covered by a net curtain on the other side. Through a slight gap he could see the corner of a narrow bed, an armchair, a TV set and a little formica table. From elsewhere in the basement swing-doors kept banging, echoing in unknown recesses. He let the water drip off his face as he listened. He dried his hands on the blue towel hanging against the yellow tiled wall, dizzy with

madness from all the yellow, from the sorrow and loneliness he'd not come to terms with in his life being bugled
right into his face. The countless toilets he had been in
during his career and it took this one, far more splendid
than some, to shake him down. Something had changed.
He envisaged Gabrielle and himself fifteen years older,
her child they had brought up together attending St
Paul's or Westminster School, a clever teenager on its
way to being a brilliant adult. And Harry would still be
going down a lavatory for pay-day.

Nothing would have made him happier at that point
than to check in his profession and take out legitimate
citizenship. But legitimate citizenship for him meant zip.
It meant state receivership. And there was no climbing
up from that.

He went to a nearby park hoping to find some people
he could sit down with. The park was busy and the
first thing he noticed was how everyone was part of a
company. He was the only solitary being. Men with long
payess spiralling out of their hats, women dressed in
wigs pushing prams, all but the youngest of children
passed him by with uniform disregard. That might have
been the kind of arrangement he normally liked, but
today he would have been happy to talk to someone.
An American in a black trilby was stopped by an old
couple asking the way to Finchley Road. The American
'didn't know the terrain'. Harry did, but wasn't
consulted. The American walked away with his ward of
English nephews and nieces and Harry was left on his
own again, watching three Yeshiva boys line up on the
grass for a race. From the very beginning the tallest of
the three runners established a big lead. He was laughing
over his shoulder at the second boy losing his yarmulka

and the fat boy who struggled just to finish. 'Well done, Epstein,' the tall boy mocked his friend trailing in last, 'you got the bronze.'

Harry did not see where he had come from, but some drink-blasted human wreck wrapped in the remnants of a raincoat that smelled of battery acid dropped on the bench beside him. Harry was about to leave him the bench when a Border Collie came running in their direction after a tennis ball. The ball was passing under the bench when the tramp trapped it with his foot. He picked up the ball and threw it. The dog swept the ball into his jaws and ran over to a man standing fifty metres away. The old tramp applauded and gave the thumbs up. Then man and dog conferred a moment. The dog ran all the way back to the bench and dropped the ball at the tramp's feet. It was an amazing trick and the dog's face was actually smiling. The tramp began to laugh. He stood up and threw the ball again. The Collie clamped the ball in his teeth and returned to his master.

It was a clever hoax, an act of friendship without commitment or dialogue. The man waved once before walking off with his dog in the direction of the Finchley Road. The tramp wanted to share his triumph. He pulled the key on his can of Tennents and took a long cele-bratory swallow. What he did next gutted Harry. The tramp offered the can to him, as if they were peers somehow, as though Harry had also been cast in that dumb little scene, as though his £1,000 charcoal-grey Dunhill suit counted for nothing at all. Harry felt such fury he slapped the can out of his hand, then ran out of the park with dozens of credit cards scratching his skin.

When he woke two hours later in that half-sleeping, half-conscious state, he believed himself to be in Gabrielle's apartment, alone and content on her bed. Then the ground listed beneath his head and the chaotic enterprise of the boat dawned all around him. He listened out for Burgess, or Simmy, but no one seemed to be around. He listened for sounds outside the boat, and heard the rumbling of construction work going on.

On the floor were sixteen credit cards stacked up in the order they were stolen, a little pile of heat growing hotter by the minute. He had come over from Golders Green to collect something and fallen asleep accidentally. In the meantime all his stolen cards had become fevered, one-dimensional objects. Stolen cards have a safe life of one to two hours after the theft. These cards from Golders Green had now been around twice that long. He didn't want to sell to Denis, because Denis was a friend, so he would have to use another fence to get rid of them.

There were other fences in town he could use, who would buy cards off him, to sell at a commission to someone else, who needed to do an hour's shopping for free. People who stole them and people who bought them were basically people on the same frequency. You had to know some people to sell them and know some people to buy them. If you tried to sell a card that was hot you'd lose at least one customer. You might also lose a couple of fingers. You couldn't fuck around with fences: they'd slice a pickpocket's fingers off with a machete to stop the guy from working again. The sixteen cards he'd acquired were now four and a half hours old. Technically he should have dumped them. But at £50 a throw it was worth the risk to try to get a price. He needed that money to buy Gabrielle's diamond bracelet.

He took all the money that he'd stashed away in the bilges of the boatman's cabin and left hastily.

He took a cab from Marylebone to King's Cross. In the Burger Bar opposite the station he passed the cards over to Benzene Smith who was frying the chips. Benzene gave him £800 in fifties and called an 0836 portable telephone number.

As Harry was stepping back onto the Euston Road, a white Porsche appeared from Gray's Inn Road and pulled up outside the Burger Bar. A black guy in a suit, six-five or taller, stepped out of the car. He had violet skin and a long, Anglo-Saxon-shaped nose, which made Harry think of ravens. He wore a strange tribal scar on his cheek. Harry could think of no instrument, blunt or sharp, that could have left that kind of mark.

Harry watched him walk in and talk to Benzene. He felt insecure about selling merchandise to strangers, which was happening more and more. So many new faces around on commission to someone else, all chasing the credit boom.

On the station forecourt Jimmy Chaucer was selling fruit and vegetables. Jimmy was a face imprinted on the mind of every dip squad in London. This meant he had to surface every other day and man the stall his mother owned outside W H Smith's. The CID could then see him doing legitimate work. He had shed his suit for a leather jacket, jeans and T-shirt to perform the menial tasks of bagging fruit, snapping crisp white paper around sprays of flowers with his diabolical craftsman's hands.

As Harry drew closer Jimmy kicked a drunken resident hooker who had stolen some of his fruit. 'What a fucking sorry bunch, Harry.' Jimmy indicated the forecourt's collection of £5 whores, lurching around in ripped tights with cans of Tennents in their fists. 'They'd steal a bucket of water from you. That's how fucked up they are.'

'You want a cup of tea, Jimmy? I'll get you one.'

In the bureau de change Harry exchanged some dollars and yen for sterling and got quite a good rate. Nothing warmed his heart more than a weak pound, high interest rates, trade deficits and inflation. He bought tea in a Wimpy, peeling off a £50 note from his roll.

Jimmy was crowded when he returned. Harry found a resting place for the teas and weighed some fruit and vegetables for him. The moment the stall became quiet again, Jimmy asked, 'Who you going to vote for in the election, Harry?'

'The election?'

'The General Election.'

'Well, I got this new girlfriend and she's Labour Party. I don't want to upset the cart over there, so I'll probably back that horse. What's the difference who you vote for, anyway?'

'What's the difference! You've got to be fucking joking! If Labour get in, they'll give all these winos and skinny fucking scrubbers jobs running the country. And one-legged black lesbians.'

Jimmy shook his head at the spectacle of teenage girls wearing yellow and turquoise mohicans on the station forecourt, selling drugs, themselves, or both.

A pimp crossed onto the forecourt from the Burger Bar. He corralled two of these girls in his arms and kissed them on the mouth. He had a bully's tiny eyes canopied beneath a swollen skull. His hair was halfway down his back. Pretty hair he'd scalped from his girls. 'Your working environment's slid down, Jimmy.'

'Another day and my mum's coming to do the stall. I'm wasted here. It's the middle of the fucking tourist season and I'm selling fucking carnations. You want to work with us again? I've had a word with Victor. He's a good boy, he listens to me.'

'I prefer it on my own.'

'Do me a favour! The last time you worked on your own you ended up getting two years. Remember?'

'I'll take my chances.'

'Ever seen that film *High Noon*? You sound just like Gary Cooper.'

Harry felt a sudden distance from Jimmy's street-talk, his crime-speak. He could see this dipper now for what he was, through Gabrielle's eyes, as a base slug. She would have no time for him, and Harry was sympathetic with that view now. Jimmy had no culture while Harry was learning all about real money and real artists like Jimmy's namesake, Geoffrey Chaucer and his book, *The Merchant of Venice*. The limit of Jimmy's scholarship was *High Noon*. 'When was the last time you went to the theatre, Jimmy?'

'The theatre? What you talking about?'

'The theatre. You know. National. The Vaudeville. Royal Bloody Shakespeare. I go there all the time.'

Jimmy laughed. 'Oh yeah? What, dipping the Gods?'

'What do you know, Jimmy?' was all Harry could manage.

'Working alone's making you a miserable bastard, Harry. Either that or you're in love.' Jimmy spotted Harry's reaction. 'You haven't fallen for that old con, have you?'

'She's an actress.'

Jimmy stretched his arms out straight, leaning his

hands against the stall for support as he guffawed, 'Oh, well, that's different then.'

Harry went red with anger. He nodded over to the whores. 'You prefer all this, do you? Low-life women. The low life doesn't interest me any more.'

Jimmy stopped laughing at him. He cocked his head, like a dog recognizing a distant whistle. Earnestly he said, 'I always thought the low life chooses *us*, Harry.'

Harry snatched an apple and bit deeply. Jimmy wrapped a few plums and presented Harry with the bag. Juice from the apple dripped on Harry's white shirt. He cursed loudly. A stain like that was a peephole into the soul of a thief. Harry poured the plums back into the cart.

'There's nothing wrong with them,' Jimmy said. 'Give them to your new girlfriend.'

'I've just stained my shirt with that fucking apple. Now you want me to carry a bag of plums around London all day. What you trying to do, ruin me?'

Harry began to move off the forecourt. He had a diamond bracelet to buy. As he crossed the Euston Road Jimmy shouted a conciliatory remark, 'Be lucky.'

Harry didn't even bother to turn around.

SEVEN

Harry bought himself a whole day out with Gabrielle with a diamond bracelet. After postponing everything he would normally be doing, they walked out along the canal tow-path from Portobello dock to Wormwood Scrubs. On her left wrist Gabrielle wore her new acquisition. She kept holding out her hand and looking at the stones set in 18 carat gold claws gleam in the sun, as if she couldn't quite believe they were real, Harry thought smugly, unaware that her real excitement had more to do with the fact that stolen money had paid for it. In the evening she was going to her parents for dinner and Harry had bought himself in there too, with the same bracelet.

As they walked arm in arm, Gabrielle kept stopping to hold her belly. 'How are you doing?' He patted her stomach, wondering when it would begin to swell. 'You know ...'

'I feel nauseous and tired. But I try not to think about it.'

'Perhaps you *should* think about it,' he hedged. 'It's growing.' Harry trembled as though he'd taken a huge jump.

Gabrielle stopped again to lay her palms on his chest. 'Of course I know I'm pregnant! If I'm trying not to think about it, it's because I'll soon have nothing else to think about. And I'll have to stop work for a while and that makes me *very* uneasy. Theatre is more than a job, it's family.' She looked into his eyes to see if he was reading her. Realizing he was at sea, she began again, patiently. 'When I'm a mother, people may not want to give me a job. I won't be one of them, you see. Childlessness is the covenant of actors. We are our own children.'

They walked for a long time without conversation. Tears ran down Gabrielle's cheeks. He felt so inadequate. He wanted to give her money. Money always cheered him up.

The vast plains of Wormwood Scrubs stretched away from the tow-path. Beyond the football pitches the floodlit towers of the prison irritated the corner of his eye. To distract himself as much as anything, he removed the silk scarf from around Gabrielle's neck and dipped a corner into the canal. Then he dabbed her swollen eyes with it. She gave in to him, raising her face to the sky. He moistened her downy facial hair and streaked her skin with black mascara.

Harry tried to conceive of himself staying indoors all day with a baby, off the harsh streets, while she went to work with her family of thespians. Contrary to his feelings about Simmy, he had no objection to making a commitment to Gabrielle's child. That would be a wise investment. It would weld their relationship. But then he caught a glimpse of himself growing pale and limp from lack of proper men's work and shook himself vigorously, like a dog climbing out of the canal.

'This was a good idea to walk along the canal. I'm feeling better already. I'm glad you are not an actor, Harry. There'd be no escape for me if you were.' She looked at his blank face. 'You don't understand what I mean, do you?'

'Isn't that the point? If I did I'd be an actor.'

'Of course! Clever man.'

Harry smiled coyly. He felt relieved to have made an impression. Ever since he'd read in a newspaper how she was considered the best theatre actress of her generation, Harry wanted someone to tell her the equivalent about him. But he wasn't even the best pickpocket of his generation. He had no laurels to rest on. 'Before I met you,' Harry brimmed with the urge to sound eloquent, 'women had been off the routine. You came along and everything tipped. That's how you know it's to the heart's advantage, isn't it?'

Gabrielle squeezed his hand, pleased by his music. But Harry had nothing more to say for himself. He had burnt himself out. Unlike Gabrielle he could not define himself with words. She discussed her work, remembered incidents in her past, at a fevered pitch. Language was important to her as a way of unlocking and enhancing experience and sharing it with others. Only when experience is moral can you do this.

Gabrielle made him aspire to something, but whenever he caught a glimpse of what that something looked like, the vision rapidly disintegrated. All he could do in the meantime was continue making money and hope another vision would burgeon out of that. No one can aspire to anything without money. Modern dreams need to be financed. To be preoccupied with poverty was more than just mind-warping and ugly. It was sinful.

When they had reached the end of Wormwood Scrubs they turned back on the tow-path. At Mitre Bridge they crossed over the water at Harry's suggestion into Kensal

Cemetery. Harry wanted to show her the tombstone of the actor Charles Kemble, so he could feel one-up on someone. But they couldn't find the grave. The high wind of the previous night had passed but its presence remained in the badly shaken trees. Under the foliage small nervous animals scuttled around.

They sat on the grass bank beside wrought-iron gates. The gates had once given access to the cemetery for waterborne funerals. Now the gates had rusted shut. The canal had a very oily texture and ceased to look like water at all, after Harry had stared into it for a while. When the sun broke through white cloud and shone on the water he could detect its muscularity under the surface. Within seconds he felt himself being tugged off, far from there.

'I had tea with Labour's shadow minister for the arts, yesterday.' Gabrielle broke into his head like a newsreader.

If he was supposed to comment he didn't. All he could manage was, 'How important is success to you?'

Gabrielle stiffened in the grass. 'What do you mean?'

'You get your face on the covers of the Sunday supplements. Politicians invite you for tea. You're very successful.'

'Is success important to you? I guess I should know already. I'm sorry I don't know what your values are. Do you think I neglect you?'

'I'm not complaining.'

'It's just that I think a little mystery is not such a bad thing. Sex feeds on it. That's why I could never get married, I think. Being married must be a bit like being celibate. We have to keep part of life a secret from each other, don't you think? Don't you think so, Harry? Do you think success is important?'

'Yeah, I do, of course I do.' Harry lowered his eyes. 'Except it's hard for me. I haven't got any skills like you have.'

'And that's painful for you, isn't it? I can see it in your eyes.'

'What you see there is envy.'

'Green is the colour of envy. Your eyes are brown.'

'The colour of shit.'

'Don't be so hard on yourself.'

'I can remember things that happened to me when I was five as if it were yesterday. They're as clear as our reflections in the water. I'm thirty-three years of age next month, halfway through my life. And I don't know what I'm supposed to be doing with the rest of it, except to do it as quickly as possible.'

She clamped her big moist hand around his neck. He felt the power of her personality in her grip and his head spun pleasantly out of control. He could not stop marvelling at her cavernous mouth. She undid the belt of her jeans and unzipped the fly right down until the rim of her white underwear showed. Then she tugged her T-shirt over her head. Harry followed a line of sweat down between her cleavage inside her bra to her stomach, folding thrice. She started kissing him, sucking his bottom lip deep into her mouth, then drew back slowly a few inches to stare at his teeth. 'Fuck me, Harry.'

'Not here.'

'Right here.'

'Someone might come along.'

'So what? Fuck me right here and now, like you've

just found what it is you should be doing for the rest of your life.' She pulled her jeans off, scratching her legs with her fingernails. He behaved so frigidly, Gabrielle had to take control to get what she wanted. Exhibitionism was her game, not his. She pulled his trousers open and then tore at her own underwear as though she hated the very feel of cotton against her skin. She mounted Harry, steering him inside. All he could see of her head was her chin. He laid his own head back and found the ground had gone. His hair dipped into the water. Gabrielle lowered her face and trembled. Harry wanted to dampen that but the deeper they kissed the more she trembled. His neck began to burn from having no support behind it. He tried to appeal to her, that he couldn't work it like this, but she was arching herself far away from him, almost in another part of the city. He reached for her nipples and pinched the little stones. Her body was silhouetted against the sky. She seized into a ball of muscle and her breasts spilled out of his hands as she barked, clear and cold, sending a flock of sparrows scuttling out of a tree. Her head crashed into his, dunking them both in the canal.

The circular oak table was screened by teak bookshelves creaking under the weight of a thousand first editions and an eight-foot-tall original painting by Clyfford Still. The books were arranged in sets: complete works of Dickens, Thackeray, Trollope. Harry preferred the abstract painting, and meditated upon blue bleeding into green. The far end of the room was a little dark but Harry could make out the shape of more paintings, carved furnishings. Sitting at the table with her parents, Gabrielle broke her uncharacteristically subdued mood to whisper to Harry an estimate on the Clyfford Still. Its value so shocked him he spent the next ten minutes devising ways to steal it.

Gabrielle's parents lived in an eighteenth-century mews house boxed in ivy. They had risen to their feet on seeing a stranger follow their daughter into the house. Harry just had time to recall Gabrielle telling him that her mother was a concert pianist before shaking hands with her across a white carpet. He trembled with jaundiced unease in case she could *feel* what his occupation was.

From his first sighting of Mr Scott, Harry could tell he ran on different fuel to the women. He was dressed immaculately in a pinstriped suit and looked as though he would rather be asleep than participate in dinner conversation. Mrs Scott was the artist and he the investment banker who brought in the bacon. The man looked exhausted to Harry. He mumbled most of the time, with his face nine inches over his soup bowl. He ate a little like Denis O'Sullivan.

After soup, Harry watched Mrs Scott toss spinach pasta with a mushroom sauce in a large Sicilian bowl. Her hands were quite beautiful; suntanned and flexible. Harry was mesmerized by the way they seemed so still, even in motion, as though under a strobe light.

The French windows were open to the garden. Outside a police car was hurrying to an incident. Harry loved the sound of that police car siren as he sat in the Scotts' house. All the trouble was out there for once and not within him.

Gabrielle had tried to dissuade him from coming tonight. But Harry had his best suit especially dry cleaned and fed her a line that if she respected him enough to consider him a potential foster parent, then she shouldn't be ashamed of him in the eyes of her parents. 'I can't remember asking you to foster any baby, Harry,' she replied.

The Scotts debated random issues and Harry lost whole conversations, while necking down the food with his head over the table. He picked up a thread when Gabrielle told them about a script she'd rejected by some garlanded director of the seventies who couldn't cut much ice with the new financiers of film productions. 'He wanted me in to make the package look commercial.'

'How much do you make for a film?' Harry asked and immediately regretted it. The question seemed too crude for the company.

'I was offered twenty thousand for this one.'

Harry clutched his fork like a dagger. 'Anything is worth doing for twenty thousand.'

'Not for this guy it's not. He killed an actor once. He made her stay naked in the North Sea in the winter, and she died of pneumonia.'

'Can you afford to turn it down?' was Mr Scott's basic question.

'Well, actually, I don't know now. I was to do *The Merchant of Venice*, but I might not be able to.'

'Good,' said Mrs Scott, placing one of her special hands behind Gabrielle's head.

'It's Shakespeare.' Mr Scott sounded puzzled. 'What's wrong with that?'

'Gabby, you haven't told your father about this?' Mrs Scott turned to her husband. 'It's going to be pruned. Shakespeare is too difficult for people to grasp nowadays, apparently.'

Gabrielle wrested her head away from her mother.

'Mummy thinks it's vandalism. I think it's pragmatic. Shakespeare is not doing so well at the box office. Simplified Shakespeare is better than no Shakespeare.'

'We *must* get tickets, Jonathan. We can't miss Portia saying, "Yo! Antonio! Well wicked, man. Give me five!" I want to hear that.'

'You're being silly, Mother.'

'I can't believe you're doing it, Gabby.'

'You have to see what they do to the text before you can say that.'

'It can't be for the money. Or maybe it *is* for the money. How much is your contract worth?'

'I'd be collecting about half a million between here and Broadway.'

'Good Lord,' Mrs Scott sighed. 'You think you know someone until someone else waves half a million in front of her face. My own daughter. Where did I go wrong? Tell me, Gabby, how did I fail? When did a million become your favourite word?'

'Mother!'

Mrs Scott addressed her next complaint to Harry. There was nowhere he could go to escape. 'This decade's seen the destruction of so many invisible things. Language is the soul of life. You start messing around with that ... I don't know. The past six or seven years has felt to me like lost time. A waste of life. It's like a prison sentence.'

'Mummy, do stop it. To say you feel like you're in prison's an insult to those who really are in gaol. I'm doing the de Vega, aren't I? That's a labour of love. I've got to make some money, too.'

Not surprisingly, Mr Scott thought that was fair.

Harry was beginning to see how Gabrielle had been

put together. Her parents' continuing support was a key element in her success. It must be a fine thing to have perceptive parents still guiding you through life's maelstroms at twenty-eight, running their fingers through your hair. She embodied both the conservatism of her father and the radicalism of her mother. With her peers in the theatre Gabrielle performed in benefits for Gays, Greenpeace, CND, the Labour Party and farted at the table. She was crusading, passionate, confrontational. All of which met with her mother's approval. Yet the body politic of her father's peers was evident in the way she advanced her brilliant career. In that area she was ambitious, individualistic, even quite ruthless. She was a frontline woman, defining the New Age morality for the rest of us.

Harry wondered how she squared all these devotions with her taste in boyfriends: a bent property developer and a pickpocket. They didn't fit in at all.

The conversation digressed four or five more times and ran for an hour and a half. Supper dialogues were still alien to Harry. The most awkward element from his point of view was the communal sharing of work experience. He sat in a state of terror in case he gave himself away. The General Election was no easier. He hadn't a clue what the election issues were. He hadn't even bothered registering to vote.

Harry felt he had nothing to offer, no common ground. He couldn't even leave £100 in cash to settle a £68 tab at the end of the meal. His money was no good here.

Then something Mrs Scott said brought him into the ring. It was a touch too excessive to his mind, what she was saying, biting the hand that fed her. Mr Scott

deserved more thanks than he got. '... the moral abso-
lute of money. Everything has been reduced to that. It's
all that families ever talk about. England's now a sick
family of molested children – destined to repeat the
cycle. Yuk!'

'They say we choose our parents ...' Harry scrambled.
He was surprised to see his remark cause confusion.

'What do you mean, exactly?'

Harry did not know what he meant, let alone exactly.
He was just passing on received information, trying to
score some points. 'I think that without predators,
society would become slothful and decadent.' He sought
out Mr Scott, looking for some back-up from him. But
Mr Scott was not in his corner. Harry ducked his head
out of their mute glares. 'Could you tell me where the
toilet is?'

'Upstairs, second door on the right.'

Harry excused himself and climbed upstairs, snarling.
He did not feel like his old self. Before he met Gabrielle
and her family, all it had taken to make him feel good
was £500 close to the skin. Gabrielle had something
intrinsic. Her parents had it too. Maybe it was hereditary, Harry considered, without knowing what it was.
If he knew what it was then he could have it too
and wouldn't feel so alienated. The way he figured
it, the difference between him and the Scotts was if
they lost all their money and their jobs tomorrow,
any bank manager would still give them a loan. When
Harry had tried to open an account a while ago the
bank refused to issue him a credit card. Harry recalled
Mrs Scott blaming the present decade for 'destroying
invisible things' and thought that was maybe why he
couldn't figure out what they had and he had missing.

It was all so mysterious and Harry hated mysteries.

Harry swept through the bedrooms upstairs, opening drawers and wardrobes. He found a jewellery box inlaid with mother of pearl gathering dust and removed a pair of gold cuff-links and a Porsche watch. He ferreted around in a frenzy. The dust off the jewellery box made him sneeze.

He sneezed again downstairs. 'Don't take anything for hay fever if I were you,' Mrs Scott said. 'There's no cure. Drugs are business schemes, not therapeutic as such.' They were sitting in the twilight end of the room, an ecumenical storage space for sixteenth-century carvings from Italian churches, Hindu wedding tables, Aboriginal dreamtime paintings. Harry choked on religious significance. He sat on a Victorian velvet sofa as Mrs Scott showed Gabrielle her new Steuben glassware displayed on the fireplace. Harry suspected she wanted a more intimate conversation with her daughter, away from Harry. But what he overheard them discuss was a public concern. 'Is the RSC really two million in the red?'

'Why do you think they keep reviving *The Taming of the Shrew*? Because the *Shrew* is an earner with tourists! *Titus Andronicus* hardly ever gets performed.'

Mr Scott lit a Turkish cigarette and threw out a challenge: 'Only one per cent of the world is cultured in the way you mean it.' He blew grey smoke out of his mouth.

Gabrielle neglected to answer. Instead she joined Harry, dropping onto the pouffe at his feet. She crossed her legs and exposed a slice of creamy white flesh above her stocking tops. Harry looked away, keeping the atmosphere holy. Mrs Scott disappeared to make coffee and Mr Scott tactfully withdrew from the room, presumably to help his wife.

Indicating the furnishings, Harry said, 'Your parents have travelled a lot ...'

'You must be joking. Everything you see in this house was bought from antique shops in Westbourne Grove.'

'They're all religious ...'

'They're the best investments.'

Harry noticed a photograph in a silver frame on the Mongolian altar table. A man posed with Gabrielle and her parents, a light aircraft on a runway behind their heads.

'Who's that in the photograph?' he asked.

'Peter Samson.'

'Do your parents like him?'

'My mother doesn't. My father does.'

'Do they know where he is at the moment?'

'Don't you read newspapers? Everyone knows where he is at the moment.'

'And that doesn't bother your father?' Harry asked. 'I mean ...'

'Peter Samson is the eighty-eighth richest man in England, according to *Business* magazine. None of it clean money. But that doesn't bother my father, no. Peter swept him off his feet, like he did me. The first time I met Peter he took me up in his light aircraft and put it into spins. I was terrified. I like men who can do that. Once he'd got inside my pants, he approached my father to bankroll one of his projects. He said the best way into a banker's pocket was with his daughter's fingers. My father calls Peter the James Dean of capitalism.'

'Your father is good at what he does ...' Harry looked around. The evidence was all there.

'But what if what he does isn't good? At least Peter *knows* he's a criminal.'

'Is your father?' What a break that would be. He had already decided Mr Scott was the kind of father he'd have chosen for himself.

'Isn't every businessman? My father's in the mergers and acquisitions department. He buys out companies for clients, who break them up, sack half the workforce just for the sake of a profit. Companies that have been family and community employers for generations. And he wants respect for it. Peter wouldn't dream of asking for respect for what he does.'

Mr Scott made a re-entry into the room, chugging along, rattling a cup in its saucer in his hand. Harry saw that he was approaching him and sat up, tensely expecting to field an incoming salvo of questions he wouldn't know how to answer. But it was his good fortune that Mr Scott was just another man in search of a listener. He leant against a white marble caryatid that supported the fireplace and held the photograph of Peter Samson with his arms around mother and father. 'Have you met Peter? Remarkable fellow. Larger than life. I did some work for him down in Bristol, before this unfortunate thing he's in. He wanted to acquire a light manufacturing plant on the Severn River. He didn't care about the plant, it was the land he was after.' He sipped his coffee in between sentences. 'I analysed the business and worked out what would be a fair price for the shares. The board of directors rejected our offer, so we made a straight tender to the shareholders and got 27 per cent. We got into a proxy fight for control of the board and Peter solicited the shareholders. I remember Peter being quite brilliant. He showed them how they'd make a 200 pence increase if he was in control. He got the requisite votes, and then some. Then he tore down the factory and put a hotel there. There was a golf course near by. A river full of salmon, or something like that. He saw the recreational value of the area before anyone else. His hotel is solidly booked all year round.'

Mrs Scott came through with a filled cafetière on a tray. 'Stop boring them, Jonathan. Why don't you two go into the garden and I'll bring your coffee out?' she offered.

Gabrielle showed Harry into the garden and they sat together on a double swing-seat, surrounded by a Dutch roofscape and ancient oak trees. 'I think you've completely charmed my parents, Harry.' She sounded as surprised as Harry was by the news. 'They're totally impressed.'

'By what?'

'Your manners ...'

'I've got terrible manners.'

'When I bring actors home they talk all night about themselves. *That's* bad manners.'

'I'd rather be charmed, like you, than charming.'

'Tell me about prison, Harry ...'

Harry knew that men who went to prison were seen by men who hadn't as exotically violent. But he didn't see the point of Gabrielle's interest.

'What's it like in prison, Harry? What's it feel like?'

'Grim. Very fucking bleak.'

'What is it like, you know, on a day-to-day basis?'

'You don't want to know that.'

'Yes, I do.'

'There is nothing really I can tell you. You're banged up twenty-three hours a day. A little association time if you're lucky.'

'What do you do for twenty-three hours in a cell?'

'Listen to medium-wave radio. *Woman's Hour* was popular. And I used to read.'

'Books?'

'I did know what a book looked like before prison,' Harry said wearily. 'I used to sit in bed fully clothed, holding my book in one hand, swapping hands under the blanket every thirty minutes to defrost.'

'Did you have to share the cell?'

'With another pickpocket.'

'Aren't they bloody geniuses, the authorities. Peter has to share a cell with this awful Pakistani bloke who is covered in boils, who shaves the top of his head like a monk because he thinks it will help his skin breathe. He can't read or write and Peter has to write all his dear sweetheart letters. "Hello, my love. How are you? I love you. Do you love me? I miss you. How are the kids? Do they miss me? I miss them. I can't wait until your next visit. How's your mother? Put her name down on the next VO if you want. Well, darling, I've got to run now. Love, Ajit." Terrible letters, Harry. Empty.'

'Americans allow rodeos inside their prisons.'

'Peter doesn't even have a view from his cell. No trees, no blossom, just the concrete yard the colour of sand. The colour of the desert.' Gabrielle put her hands behind her head and thoughtfully studied Harry's profile. 'You know, Harry, and I know you'll think this is crazy, but sometimes I think I wouldn't mind swapping life experience with you and Peter. I've had it so good. Sometimes I'm short of things to draw on. And that frightens me. Your lives have been a real test of character.'

'What you want is the experience of a thief without the consequences.'

'That's precisely what acting is.'

'Then I wouldn't mind being an actor. Who needs consequences!'

Mrs Scott entered the garden with coffee and mint chocolate pieces on a tray. Gabrielle waited until she returned to the house before staring at Harry expectantly. She dunked her mint chocolate into her coffee and Harry ate his straight. An essence of mint filled his head, clearing his sinuses. 'Do your parents know about your life in London?'

'My parents aren't like yours. They're out of the picture for one thing.'

'Tell me about your childhood.'

'Hell, no.'

'Go on.'

'What's the point? I don't see the point of it.'

'The point is, you're suppressing a natural instinct. Everybody needs to exercise their memory. Children want to remember what they did yesterday. Old men want to remember their childhoods. As long as you have memory you have life. Dimension. Even if the memory is painful, it is better to recall than to bury it. One buries the dead.'

'I don't know how to.'

'Let me help you. Your house ... where was your bedroom?'

'What?'

'Where was your bedroom, as a child?'

'I didn't have a bedroom. I slept on a sofa.'

'What colour was the sofa?'

'What do you want to know that for?'

'Just answer me.'

'Green, I think. Greeny-brown.'

'Two-seater, three-seater ...?'

'Christ, Gabrielle ... Two, with a dip in the middle. It had wooden arms.'

'Where did your parents sleep?'

'They didn't sleep together. They both had a drink problem. He slept in the kitchen.'

'Is your father dead?'

'He'd drink all night and smash things up a bit, go into the kitchen. Then I'd make my bed on the sofa. In the morning he'd reappear, stepping round the debris, wake me up, rub his hands together like a schoolboy and say, "I'm going to make some nice bacon and eggs now." By nine he'd be pissed again.'

'What was the wallpaper like in the room?'

'The *wallpaper*? Jesus ... patterned with little country cottages, horses and carts.'

'What about the carpet?'

'That was patterned too, with red flowers.'

'What did the room smell like?'

'Booze, cigarettes, like a pub ...'

Without warning Harry was jerked by the neck into the past, into that room, eating a plate of sardines off his lap, his eyes glazed and jaw slack from having watched a straight six hours of television. Wedged on the sofa with him was the mute carcass of his mother, undoing her knitting as she did every night in order to start all over again.

He suddenly shivered uncontrollably as his father threw cold, soapy washing-up water over him from a basin. Harry was twelve years old, in his pyjamas, and his father was waking him up for school. He could hear the voice of Frank Sinatra singing on the radio 'What is This Thing Called Love?' His nostrils filled with a terrible smell, like rotting fruit fermenting. 'Christ!' Harry gagged on it. 'God almighty!' He felt for the arms of the sofa. A familiar picture began to take shape above the mantelpiece: a Woolworth Messiah at Calvary with a tear forming in the corner of his big blue eyes stared down at him. He heard a sound of crashing. He tried to get up from the swing-seat, step out of his wet pyjamas. But his pyjamas came with him. He found his mother in the kitchen, attempting something vigorous in the darkness. He flicked on a switch and bathed the tiny kitchen in harsh light. His mother was hunched over the fridge, her arms rigid in front of her. A bottle rolled across the floor and beer ran down the walls, dripping from her hair and face. She was breathing like an over-exerted athlete. She stared into an inch of beer in two glasses, as though trying to remember a dream. Coloured light shone into the window from the street, falling on her face, turning it orange one side, lemon on the other, her hair green. She was standing on a newspaper that ripped slowly under her weight. On the radio, Sinatra continued to sing: 'Last night when we were young, love was a star …' His mother was trying to sing along, but what came out of her mouth was nonsense. The crescent scar across the bridge of her nose had reopened and was bleeding. There were heavy black marks etched under her eyes and her stomach was distended like a balloon. She was kindling: barren and dry. His mother ran past him into the living-room. Harry went after her to see her fly straight into the wall like a trapped bird. 'Hey!' Harry stopped her from doing it again and carried her to the bedroom. The bedside table was littered with bottles of pills, cigarette packets. After Harry lowered her onto the bed she propped her back against the silver plastic headboard and struggled to find the words to keep him there. 'I want you to stay with me ...'

Harry began to weep. Tears sprang out of his eyes. He could not remember the last time he cried. He was on his feet with Gabrielle beside him, trying to coax him back onto the swing-seat. Gabrielle had set him up. She had played some trick on Harry, applied some actor's method which left him naked.

Mr Scott was calling from inside the house, offering them a liqueur. Gabrielle stopped him short of the French windows. 'We'll continue this later,' she said.

Harry pulled his arm free. 'No way. You've got the basic story. You've got the drift. I'll explode if I tell you more.'

'It's good to talk about it.'

'It's too easy for you to say that.'

In the house, Mr Scott lay across a maroon sofa with his chin in the palm of his hand. Mrs Scott was playing on the Steinway. Harry looked up to where Mr Scott stared blissfully at the ceiling, hoping that he too would find a state of ecstasy up there. He wanted to be set free. But all he could see was a horsefly trapped in the lamp shade, roasting in the heat of the bulb.

He excused himself to go to the bathroom. He reached the moiré silk hallway but knew he would never make the stairs. He was splitting apart. He opened the front door and stepped into the street.

Harry took a vigorous piss ten yards from the house

in the leafy heartland of Hampstead. So satisfying was it that when a woman walked past with a small dog on a leash, he stood his ground and kept up the flow against a lichen-covered wall.

Harry tracked down an image of his mother from the last time he had seen her, living alone in a single-berth caravan in Newport docks. His father had died the year before. She was a useless shell, her old Welsh drawl like the song of the dead. She was living on the Social, hobbling on the banjo, lost in time, glad to get each day over. *Her* art collection consisted of a picture of the Queen Mother pasted to the plywood wall, torn from a tabloid newspaper. The Sellotape holding it on was grubby with her fingerprints. She sat in the caravan each day, looking at the Queen Mother, serenaded by the popping and groaning of polypropylene ships' hawsers tightening around mooring bollards.

If she could see Harry now. Except that would never be possible. She would ruin everything.

EIGHT

Every time he thought about the money he was letting go by, he cringed a little. This was the second day of work he had forfeited at £500 a day. But his discomfort was compensated by the well-being he got riding shotgun in Gabrielle's 18v GTI. It had been her idea to travel to the west coast, to his childhood home. Following their conversation in her parents' garden, she now wanted to see a pickpocket's habitat.

She drove for the two hundred miles as Harry described what their destination, a small sea-town in the west, would look like: a nexus of pre-war pubs, fresh produce market, rugby ground, gasworks, steelworks and docks – all dusted in drifting sand. A busy parochial town of headstrong women, dockers, seamen, colliers.

Five hours later, driving through that same town, Gabrielle had a job connecting the Mega Store Video, Toys Я Us, Plantasia, drifting across the windscreen, with Harry's descriptions of the place. She crawled through the docks in second gear. Its ships, gantries, sailors had all been replaced by a red-brick marina with private yachts and a solitary nineteenth-century merchant clipper imprisoned in an enclosed basin. 'It looks like anywhere in England, Harry,' she complained, making him feel culpable. 'Just another place where you're supposed to get high staring at other people's wealth.'

Another twenty miles on and she became mollified by the rural peninsula. 'It's like my play. Look ... farmers.' He just wanted to go in and out the same day, returning to London before nightfall. He wished to avoid running into someone he knew, ordinary sentinels Gabrielle would think dull. Ideally he wouldn't have got out of her German car. But Gabrielle spotted the sea embracing the peninsula and urged him to walk around for a while.

Every feature of the peninsula was unnervingly familiar to him: the sheep-nibbled grass, isolated smallholdings, sightings at long distances of men working the land, vessels under full sail inhaling the wind. Harry let his feet go down well-known paths between hedgerows and fields lying fallow. A smell of heather and burnt grass perforated the rich ozone. Salt-blast made his skin tingle. A hang-glider under an orange rig coasted over the field with a large buzzard flying alongside. They watched the bird break off formation and freefall like a stone and roll a tiny rabbit in the field. The buzzard steamed the creature and dismembered it with his beak. Then the buzzard raised his head and screamed. The performance shocked Gabrielle, who kissed Harry violently, transferring that emotion into sexual energy. The hang-glider tacked over the sea and sliced the sky above, using the thermals from a flock of sheep to gain altitude.

The fields gave way to limestone rock smeared with patchy grass. The footpath vanished at the rock face. He pointed to the skeletal ribs of the bullion ship sticking out of the sand below, shipwrecked in the last century. Local farmers looted the ship and bought the freehold to their land in gold. Harry regretted not being a descendant of those thieves: his father was a poor labourer. There had been many other shipwrecks off this coast, but none had brought in any bounty. The sea was steel grey, folding over the sand every few seconds in tiny, perfect waves. The sight of it calmed him immediately.

Harry remembered bigger, shipwrecking waves and how he used to surf them. Surfing was an apt obsession for a lonely boy, connected to nothing except the power of the sea. He suggested to her how brave he was: when thirty-foot boats with VHF and radar went straight into harbour, he would be half a mile out at sea on a seven-foot fibreglass surfboard, getting high on a gale force eight. 'Big waves are glamorous,' he said. 'They glitter and run fast.'

'You must be a strong swimmer,' she said.

'I'm not afraid of the sea.'

The beach was called Langland. When Harry vanished to London he changed his surname to Langland as a form of disguise but also to remind himself of all the wasted years watching the tide come in and out, watching his skin darken in the sun.

The peninsula was one of the most westerly outposts in Britain. You couldn't escape any further west, except to the holy isles – the burial grounds of medieval saints. On a clear day you could see the islands rising out of the Irish Sea, like hunchbacks or rats. As a young man he resented their existence. At that age he wanted to be far away from sacramental grounds of the dead.

At certain places the cliff had been hollowed by the sea, reducing the path to a crumbling ledge overhanging a hundred-foot drop. He snatched Gabrielle's hand as they walked across these places. 'A million families have walked this path. It could go any minute. How quickly we can die.'

'How brief is rapture?' Gabrielle remarked.

They left the treacherous footpath and cut through the fields again to where the car was parked outside a chapel. Ewes and their lambs were grazing in the field. Some of the lambs were just a few days old, their legs collapsing as they tried to run. Gabrielle was enchanted. She placed a hand on her belly and felt attuned to the natural world. Five metres on she slipped in placenta in the grass and her legs split across a lamb's warm corpse, its tongue ripped out.

Harry comforted her in his arms. 'Magpies rip out the tongue when the lamb's born. It can't feed then, so it starves to death. The ravens come along and pluck the eyes from the corpse.'

'Ah! Harry! For God's sake!'

'It's dog eat dog in the country.'

He steered her into the chapel cemetery where his father's grave was lost in the grass. He looked for a spot where alcohol fumes might be rising from the earth. He said nothing about his father to Gabrielle and stepped on the thought. The grass was spongy underfoot like a thick carpet. From the chapel he could see Dungannon Park, an estate on a hill where the council housed problem families. Whenever people from the peninsula used to drive through there they'd lock their car doors. It acquired mythical status from all the bad trouble it contained. Only once did it flood out that Harry could remember. A gang came to the peninsula and attacked the men on Langland beach with bicycle chains and razor blades sewn into handkerchiefs. Harry watched from behind a rock, felt witness to something truly satanic as they climbed back up the hill with steam rising off their backs. It wasn't until he'd been to prison that he realized evil was more mundane, in the routine way it takes place.

They sat on a bench in the graveyard beneath flowering cedar, whitebeam and yew. Gabrielle was happy. The peninsula was benign. Young mothers pushing prams up the lane represented freedom to her. To Harry they looked crude and obvious, and as sexless as he imagined sisters to be.

Dungannon Park, reflecting in the windows of her car, was dreamy and absorbent with a wisp of cumulus hanging over the slate roofs. At one stage she had to make a call from her car phone and Harry heard her saying, 'I'm at the seaside having a great time. In among the ruins and the wild life.'

As night fell they took their London sandwiches into the chapel, a simple whitewashed building with thick bare stone walls and slate roof, like a barn with rather fine oval windows. Gabrielle read from a chapel booklet how the Normans had conquered the peninsula in the twelfth century and established its first church. The chapel was built on the ruins by Britons displaced to western outposts by invaders. During the Middle Ages the peninsula became a home for holy men who came to die there. Paradise was thought to be in the west. Outposts jutting into the sea were springboards into the afterlife.

'I know all that,' Harry snapped. 'I did live here, you know.'

'I can feel a connection to the past just sitting here.'

'I never want to live in the past.'

Gabrielle ate the sandwich Harry couldn't finish. He lost his appetite the moment they arrived.

A modest altar stood in the chancel and the roof beams were exposed. Working late, two men were erecting scaffolding inside, while another few consulted architect's plans and stretched a measuring-tape around the walls. The developers harboured a thinly veiled intolerance for the handful of people sitting in the pitch-pine seats, their heads dipped in prayer.

Harry had never gone in for chapel at any time in his life. He felt uneasy being in one now and persuaded Gabrielle to leave.

Harry led the way into the dark, trying to shake out a cooing in his head. It sounded too much like a baby. But Gabrielle also heard the noise, present throughout the peninsula. A little prodding around in his memory produced the answer and he told Gabrielle about colonies of Manx shearwaters returning from feeding in the Irish Sea, how they made up an evening's raft, calling and answering their partners in the nests. They returned in darkness, he added, to thwart the seagulls, who would kill them if only they had light to see.

Then a full moon rolled into the sky and the shearwaters became silent. The peninsula seemed to rise with the moon, like an ark on flood waters. In the moonlight a woman evolved spectrally in the graveyard, followed by three small children carrying flowers in their arms. She was in her thirties now, like Harry, who recognized her with a jolt. Her name was Sheena. Twenty years ago they had sat side by side in the village school. As she approached, the weight of Gabrielle's hand on Harry's arm lightened until he could no longer feel her with him. He made eye contact with Sheena and smiled at the memory of her as a teenager walking across the sand in four-inch stilettos. Sheena averted her face as if he were just another predatory male and walked straight past him to attend her family grave. Harry was shaken. Had he altered so much? Was there nothing of the past recognizable in him?

NINE

The air in Gabrielle's flat felt heavy and portentous, like some burglar had been and gone. Harry gently closed the front door behind him and walked into the lounge. A box of her autographed photographs was spewed across the floor among issues of *Plays & Players* and television scripts. One of two Turkish mirrors framed in pewter had been smashed. Shards of silvered glass on the parquet floor transmitted his own broken image back to him. In the surviving mirror on the wall he saw another head bobbing around behind his own, like a buoy cut from its moorings, bodiless and adrift. He stood there unable to react to the image he'd first seen in a photograph. The distinctive streak of grey in the fringe of black hair jogged the memory. Harry jerked his head round so fast it filled his eyes with mist.

'You're Peter Samson, aren't you?' Harry received neither confirmation nor denial. The man seemed happy riding on the protracted pause, giving nothing away. The stress was all on Harry to part with information. He was the thief who had to explain his presence there. 'I am a friend of Gabrielle's.'

'A friend with a key ...'

'I've seen your picture. She showed me a picture of you.'

'And who are you?'

'Harry ...'

'Where is Gabby?' His voice was calm, authoritative. His body was leaning, about to dive, betraying the unease his voice tried to conceal. He seemed out of sync, as though he'd just stepped off an aircraft from the other side of the world.

'I don't know ...' Harry considered Samson's turtle-neck sweater which rambled all over his torso. His corduroys were faded and baggy at the knee. Harry felt the more secure for being in a suit.

'That makes two of us then.' He had a soft face, big chin and big hands. Fleetingly Harry imagined him as Gabrielle's lover and quickly strangled the thought. His hair had grown over his ears and flicked up at the collar. 'I could do with a drink. I don't know what kind of day you've had, but I've just parted with two million pounds for bail. I wonder if Gabby still has my liquor.'

Harry's face was burning hot as he followed Samson around, trying to imagine what it would be like to carry a couple of million pounds in cash. What couldn't fit into a briefcase was beyond the scope of his imagination. Two million would need a truck, he reckoned, perhaps even several trucks. He couldn't help thinking how he'd done eighteen months' bird for stealing a wallet containing twenty pounds, while Samson had been able to get out by paying the court two million good ones. The sheer amount involved seemed to lend Samson an aura, like a film star.

In the kitchen Samson opened a cupboard door. 'Here it is.' He excavated a bottle of expensive malt from behind a sack of organic oatflakes. 'I knew I had a bottle somewhere.' He took two glasses off the draining-board next to the sink and half filled each glass with whisky.

'I've been dreaming of malt whisky. I've seen it poured into a tumbler in my sleep.' He handed one to Harry and clinked the glasses together. 'Chin-chin.'

'What do you think of the décor in this kitchen? Nice, isn't it? I got the most expensive interior designer in London to do it as a birthday present.' Samson had a strange accent, suggesting layers of different cultures and histories. Harry thought he detected an East End twang at one point, from around Manor Park.

Harry raised the glass to his lips and was astounded by how smooth the malt tasted. He glanced back at the chaos of broken mirror and A4 paper in the lounge. 'When I first saw you standing in here I thought you might have escaped from prison.'

'Oh no, although I did discover a way. Have you ever been inside?'

'Where?'

'If ever you have to do time, Harry, enrol in an evening-class. Study English and escape through the class system.'

'The what?'

'Prison teachers make staggered entrances into the building of an evening, checking their names in at the main gate. But they never get checked *out*, aren't even counted. That seems arse backwards to me. Who wants to break *into* a prison? Teachers are above suspicion, I suppose. Too dull to be anything other than what they seem.' Samson poured another inch of malt into his glass. 'If you asked me what the key to my success has been, I'd say it was seeing chances no one else has seen before. How many people have broken out of prison posing as a teacher, do you think?'

'You haven't told me how yet.'

'Ah. Well, you bribe a warden to hide civilian clothes in the room where your class meets.'

'You'd need money for that.'

'I'm afraid that's true. Very hard to get up from the floor without money. It's true. But let's assume that you have some. You bribe a warden. Then when the classes wrap and everyone goes into the corridor to be searched, you get under a table and put these clothes on top of your uniform. There's over sixty men pushing and shoving in the corridors, right, and all the screws are busy with them. Then you walk straight into the line-up of teachers at the back door. They get ushered out very quickly into a courtyard. You cross the courtyard in the dark. Then the two security gates where nobody checks you out.'

'And that's it?'

'That's it.'

'Wouldn't the teachers know each other? They might know you.'

'They come in for an hour a week. Seven or eight of them. They don't know each other well, if at all. You'd do this in the winter, you understand. When it's dark.'

Harry was quite taken by his relaxed charm. Samson was so communicative and warm, all the more remarkable considering where he'd been festering for the past twelve months. They had only just met and were already discussing very personal things. Harry wanted to ask him the last question first – how did you get rich? – but he managed to contain himself.

The whisky went straight to Harry's head and made him feel sentimental. So many good things were opening up for him. Here he was in the home of one of the nation's leading actresses, sharing a malt with the eighty-eighth richest man in England, who was living proof of the regenerative power of money. Samson had come out of prison, smiling and asking for whisky. Knowing he had money to come out to had kept him fresh in the mind. Harry felt a pang of guilt for cheating on him, *vis-à-vis* Gabrielle, but his guilt was thin as their acquaintance was brief. He had no way of telling for sure how things would pan out when Gabrielle turned up, but for the moment he felt his life being enriched twofold.

They both heard Gabrielle's car pull into the drive. Harry followed Samson up from the table and to his feet, with whisky in hand, as the key turned in the front door. Gabrielle saw Samson, took a glancing look at the broken mirror and threw all her bags into the air. Emitting a loud yelp she exploded onto the scene in the kitchen.

She was more vibrant than Harry had ever seen her before, turning the room into a storm. Her soft syllables whistled as they hit the gap in her teeth. 'Peter! You got bail? Thank God! What a relief.' She ignored Harry completely to smother the cuckold. Harry was too impressed by her stagecraft to feel jealous. She was a cool head, the way she dealt with her infidelities. Pure theatre of disguise.

She began stalking up and down the room, crying out in happiness. Her delivery was superb, each phrase timed for maximum effect. She even spoke in rhyming couplets a few times. It occurred to Harry she was bringing the experience of the stage into their life at home. Maybe she'd even use the experience of their life together on stage one day.

Gabrielle began to cry. Samson touched her cheek.

She turned her head away from his gaze and Harry watched her catch a reflection of herself in the surviving Turkish mirror. She stayed completely still for a long moment, examining her profile, interested to see what she looked like in this state. She filed it away in her memory for some future role, then addressed Harry in the mirror, just like she had the first time he'd met her in the theatre. 'Harry, leave us now, there's a love. We've got so much to talk over. Peter must be exhausted after his ordeal. Stay in touch, won't you?'

TEN

For three days he never left the boat. He drilled holes into the steel roof, tapped and died them ready to take a new bulkhead frame; painted the water tank and inside the hull below the waterline with bitumen; fitted battens and sawed timber for floorboards, screwing them into the battens; made portholes adapted from sheet glass, using steel-piercing drills and jig-saws with fierce energy. He laboured hard to lose himself.

At night after the builders went home, Harry and Burgess entered the construction site and stole several bags of Rockwool insulation to lag the cabin and hauled out two and a half tons of paving-stones for ballast. As a youth, Harry had been employed briefly by a boat builder. He was pleased to find his skills had not deserted him, while wondering where Burgess got hers.

Burgess had atmosphere, like Gabrielle, although the two women couldn't have been more different. Gabrielle's atmosphere was borne out of acquisition, Burgess's from victory over deprivation. Her face had many tiny scars, the stigmata of hard times. They had hardened into purple cicatrices and set off her features, like jewellery set off Gabrielle's. She did not vex Harry as Gabrielle did. Burgess was disenfranchised and Harry never felt threatened, dull or minor. He didn't need to perform for her. Everything he said was easy.

In three days they accomplished what Burgess, on her own with the baby, would have taken weeks to do.

He ran back and forth to Simmy whenever she screamed for attention. Her cries got right through to him each time, as if he'd known her all along. He'd pick her up gently around the waist to hold her in front of his face. There was nothing more comical than Simmy crying. She went stiff from exertion and pink in the face. She had pixie ears, no hair and no teeth. The more she cried, the more Harry laughed at her. She bared her gums like an old man, her tiny fingers searching his face for handles and excavating his mouth. To pacify her he usually took her up on deck to see what interesting things they could watch floating on the water. She would stop crying and begin snorting, cooing, whoo-ing. The range and tone of her soprano was the thing he liked most. She said 'here' and 'uh-huh' and 'tzah' and 'oerr ...' She made sounds like a seabird. Did seabird songs mean anything? Several times she would look at him as though she recognized a man in trouble.

In order to give Simmy time to drop off to sleep in the afternoons they would stop work for ten minutes and sit in the front cabin next to her cot. Burgess would cook up a brew of tea.

'It's nice to have you around for longer than five minutes, Harry. There's nothing wrong, is there? You haven't stepped off this boat in days.'

'Nor have you,' Harry deflected. 'Don't you ever want to go out sometimes? Take the baby into town?'

'The city does my brain in. I don't feel safe there.'

Harry knotted his forehead in the same way Gabrielle would do when squeezing out a lump of polemic. He had remembered something important. 'Denis O'Sullivan told me the police found another leg floating in the canal.'

'Yeah, I know. I dreamt the other night that leg was mine. *They* had caught up with me and cut me into little pieces.'

'So how come you feel safe here?'

'The leg was only *found* in the canal. That doesn't mean he was murdered here. He was probably duffed up in Threadneedle.'

'Well, I'm getting restless sitting here all day long. I need to get out a bit.'

'I don't.'

'At least you know what you *don't* want,' Harry remarked cynically. 'We all have to start somewhere.'

'What about you, Harry? Do you know what you don't want?'

'I know what I *want*.'

'What?'

Harry looked at her disparagingly for asking such an obvious question. People who live underground do not know what's in the air. He blasted her with self-evident truths: 'Money. I told you before ... I don't want to have to worry about anything. Money gives you all you need to stand out in a crowd. I want to walk into a restaurant and hear my name on men's mouths. I want to be looked up to. I want to be envied.'

Harry stared through a porthole to catch his breath. He reached into his trouser pocket and took out some old bank notes that had stuck together. He separated the £10 and £5 notes, careful not to tear them. There was not much cash left in his trousers. He often wondered how he managed to spend everything. He bought expensive clothes, drinks all round, and more recently a few things for Gabrielle. When people asked him what he earned, he'd usually tell them around £500 a day. But that couldn't be right. He certainly wasn't *spending* £500 a day. He had conned himself somehow, or hadn't been working enough, occupied with Gabrielle when he had the chance, preoccupied with her when he didn't.

He laid £25 down for Burgess.

'I don't want it.'

'Don't give me this grief again. You can't convince me, living in these conditions, that you need nothing. Nothing is a yellow streak down your trousers.'

Her laughter drove his anger deeper. Then the baby woke and laughed at him too.

Burgess finished painting a name for the boat on a slab of quarry slate, drilled at either end. It was to be called *Irish Jack* after the man outside, a fifteen-stone alcoholic who stood in pubs all day catching other men's eyes, then whacked them round the temples with his fist. The only kindness he'd ever shown was for Burgess, acting as her midwife, bringing her food from the Salvation Army. She hoped his name would bring the boat luck. By the law of nature, Irish Jack should have been dead by now.

Before the paint had dried, Burgess crouched on the stern and attempted to drill two holes in the transom to take the plate. Harry was inside the cabin trying to stare out the baby, when he heard a loud splash. He waited a second. 'Burgess?' He looked at the baby, who turned her head towards the cabin door, deep in thought. Harry went out on the aft deck where he saw concentric wakes rolling across the surface of the water, away from the boat. Burgess was missing. His knees bent automatically and his lungs sucked in air ready to spring off the side, when Burgess broke the surface. She stood up in three feet of water, brushing the hair out of her face, blinking, trying to figure how she'd gone from the boat to the water so quickly. Harry knelt on the gunwale and stretched out his hand. He grabbed her crooked fingers and levered her back on board. 'I was just about to dive in after you.'

'You'd have hit your head on the bottom.'

'I forgot how shallow it is.'

'Well, I know where the bottom is now and it's disgusting. I couldn't see anything. It was all slimy and horrible.'

'It won't be the last time you fall in, I expect.'

'So what? I can swim.'

'A lot of people drown even though they can swim. It lulls them into thinking they're invulnerable in water. But water can freeze you to death. It can suck you down. Water has no guilt.'

'This isn't the sea, Harry, or a tidal river. It's just a boring old canal.'

'There are weirs and locks on canals, aren't there? As soon as your baby's old enough you should give her some lessons in how to survive them. Even boring old canals can take lives.'

'You should be a lifeguard instead of a thief.'

'If you had drowned, that baby would be an orphan already. You got to consider these things, Burgess. Water is no friend to anyone. It lives alone, it doesn't care.'

'If I drowned I would hope that Simmy's father would come out of the bushes and take care of her.'

'You do believe in miracles, don't you?'

Burgess started the engine to charge up the batteries.

It made a low thumping sound and woke up the winos from their stupor. With the engine running she was able to use the new water-pump and fill the stainless steel sink, acquired from the building site, and give Simmy her first bath since she was born.

With the kid shrieking in the sink, lumps of plaster and bricks kept hailing down on the cabin roof. Burgess shared a look of concern with Harry. Soon the construction workers would be coming to fill in the basin under the warehouse for a car park. The final stages of the boat's conversion would take her another few months, but she could set sail in it now if she had to. She declared that tonight she was going to take the boat out on a maiden voyage a mile up the canal and back.

Harry decided it would be a good time for him to join the world again.

Irish Jack appeared on the tow-path near the front cabin as Burgess was untying the ropes. He was crying silently. Burgess looked at him for a moment before handing him the freshly bathed Simmy. The Irishman was dressed in dirty blue jeans and an old black leather sports coat. He sat with Simmy on a stool that had found its way under the warehouse and pressed the baby's pink bald head gently into his blackened, unshaved face. He rocked back and forth on the stool, creaking from his weight.

She made a very casual exit from the warehouse basin. The engine filled the air with agricultural diesel smoke. It was loud, but it was music. The Russell Newbery had a slow two-beat rhythm like a talking drum. She backed the boat out of the warehouse with the baby lying in a cot on the cabin roof.

Harry led the three Celts over the piles of cardboard

and out of the building to see Burgess turn what now seemed like a steel chrysalis under the cranes and scaffolding. It was raining heavily. The site labourers had all gone home. She brought the boat around and gave herself more throttle, covering the baby's cot with a tarpaulin sheet. The winos bundled together on the tow-path were hardly aware of what was happening outside their heads, until Burgess turned at the tiller and blew them a kiss. Then they knew. They cheered the sight of one of their own coming out into daylight, moving with a sense of direction they had lost a long time ago. The boat's rudder churned the brown water into a heap of leaves and mud.

He looked up into the rain. Burgess's arm was hooked around the tiller, her face set against the weather. Within a minute she had left the basin and was entering a short tunnel. Her hair was smooth against her scalp, the wet plastic shoulders of her donkey jacket shining like black ice. Then the tunnel enveloped her and it all went silent. He waited for a while, half expecting her to return. But only a grey-brown cloud of smoke the colour of her hair issued back out of the tunnel mouth, rising into the air like a signal of goodwill before dispersing in the rain.

As night fell Harry walked into the conveniences and inhaled that persistent smell of urine which always reminded him of pay-days. He opened the door to the attendant's private cubicle. Inside the table was littered with silver paper, bent teaspoons, polythene bags, burnt matches, ink remover, Tipp-Ex, candles, tobacco shreds. Denis was asleep on the floor, lying on his back, gargling saliva. He sat up sharply when Harry flooded the room with the overhead strip-light.

Harry needed a drink. Denis knew where you could go and drink after hours. It was to that kind of place they journeyed. With Denis at the steering-wheel of his Escort they cruised around a shanty town in the Hackney area, a piece of Third World London Harry normally tried to avoid.

His hopes that they were passing through were dashed when Denis pulled up under a railway bridge. A curtain of water poured off the bridge and played a timpani on the bonnet. They got out and began to walk. Every piece of architecture around them was an aggressive un-compromising shape; rusting steel or shattered black brick crowned with broken glass, dulled by night. LAMI-NATING, WELDING, PANEL-BEATING were the words of welcome etched into padlocked doors. The streets were littered with spent missiles and burnt-out autos. Whole terraces of Victorian houses had been gutted and fires burnt in empty lots. Traffic lights changed from red to green, green to red at silent windswept junctions.

'Where is this place, Denis?' Harry asked.

'Not far.' He led the way down a street that looked blitzed. Harry stepped around piles of bricks that had been heaved into the road and realized why they had to leave the car so far away. Charcoaled edifices, walls of corrugated tin rolled by. They cut across a gaunt mod-ern estate, carpeted with broken glass and floodlit to inhibit residents from assaulting each other. In the spill of the light, Harry spotted the canal running inexorably beyond the steel-mesh fence surrounding the estate. They were back on Regent's Canal again. The water looked a soft and gentle creature caged behind the fence. He wondered whether the fence was designed to keep the canal away from the estate or if it was the other way round.

Denis stopped at the corner house of a terrace backing on to the estate. The sky above was tinted red, turning green then yellow, perforated by twists of reggae. A muslin sack parted across a first-floor window: Red fingernails on the window-frame, an outline of Afro-hair, a face in darkness. 'Here,' said Denis, 'this is the gaff.'

The front door sprang open, drawing them into a hall littered with carrier bags, unsolicited mail. A curtain over a door-frame parted and the light from this room marginally brightened their passage through. They stepped into a modest-sized living-room with a cold fireplace and wallpaper interior, lit overhead by a single orange bulb. A black woman in a brunette wig sat with a girl of secondary school age. She kept lifting up her pink vest straps that slid down her narrow shoulders. They were perched at a makeshift bar, a chipboard surface lying on two tea chests. The bar looked as portable as the females. A couple of pot-bellied thugs made an entrance from an adjoining room and asked Denis for £5 'tax' per head. Denis gave them the money and the woman passed them two glasses decorated with diamond transfers and a bottle of cheap blended scotch, which Harry paid for, at three times its retail price. The two other men sat on stools each side of the girl and ran their hands up her back under the vest. She drank from their glasses and convulsed each time.

Harry no longer drank like he used to, but now and again when he'd made up his mind, he did drink like he used to. Then there was no such thing as one drink. He went at it until everything coiled out of focus. It flattened out the bottom, quietened the ructions in his head. He and Denis had different private reasons for wanting to drink, and to drink deeply. There was no covenant between them, little conversation. They worked on the bottle as an act of labour, not an act of love.

The last thing Harry remembered doing before losing consciousness was babbling about Gabrielle to the black woman, who varnished her nails throughout his testimony. 'I love you. I'd die for you right now. I'll kill myself. I love you to death. When I'm with you I don't want to be anywhere else, do anything else, I never want to see anyone or share you with anyone. I want the world to disappear. God help me. I'm doomed. You don't love me at all. I love you and you don't love me. If I could fly an airplane and go into spins I bet you would love me ...'

Harry woke like a corpse casually resurrected in a strange place. He tried to establish links with his environment until he recognized the house piece by piece. The woman and the young girl were sleeping in armchairs, the two proprietors gone. Harry tried to lift his head off the bar and immediately felt sick. The room began to spin around him. He caressed his stomach in circular motions, focusing his eyes on Denis's shoes on the ground.

By the time he was able to sit up straight it was dawn. He found himself on the floor next to Denis, who had also come to and was shaking his head. Both armchairs were empty and the bar had been packed away and removed. Harry looked around at the muddy carpet, at the wallpaper peeling off the walls, and longed to be in Gabrielle's arms, sucking her gold earrings. Through the window, black skeletal shapes of high-rise blocks of flats dug into the deep-blue sky.

He and Denis walked out of the house. They retraced their steps across the estate back to where the car was parked. Denis sat at the wheel trying to steady his vision, breathing through one nostril and exhaling through the other. He turned the engine over and stalled the car. He had left the handbrake on. Harry's dipper hands sat on his lap like stones. Denis turned the key again with too much toe on the pedal and the car screamed back at him. He jerked the clutch and the car shot forward. Everything seemed possible to Harry, now they were moving.

Denis pulled the car over abruptly. 'I can't see the road, Harry. I can't see fuck all.'

'Let's walk.'

They say that Hackney has become full of unemployed white intellectuals sitting around in coffee bars discussing the influence of monetarism on modern jazz. Harry saw none of this as he and Denis invaded the street, trying to locate the canal on foot. Perhaps they'd all found jobs and moved away. He didn't want to see the place again either, with its entire infrastructure wheezing and creaking. It felt like a punishment to be there, in a little town twinning with some African shanty.

They rediscovered the canal as the early morning sun was tinting the water crimson. Mist rose from the water, rose from their skins. Shimmering lorries crossed a bridge, their engines droning in Harry's ears like the sound of surf in a seashell. Harry couldn't feel his body, hear his footfalls as they staggered like ghouls along the tow-path. He bought ice-creams from a petrol station to fill their stomachs and soak up the alcohol. The few people around at that time of morning gave Denis a wide berth. The tattoos on his luminous white skin looked particularly sinister in the early morning light. But as long as Harry could remember Denis sucking a raspberry ripple, he would never be frightened of him.

Harry got down on his knees at one point to trail a finger in the water. He recalled that leg found by divers. Had someone drowned in the canal, or, as Burgess suggested, been thrown in after a killing? There was no need for such deaths by drowning. Burgess was right, he should have been a lifeguard. He stared into the water, visualizing that leg until he got a sense of the whole person it belonged to. The body, he decided, was female. Harry performed an imaginary resurrection of nature, saving this girl from drowning. He looked across the water to the far bank and watched her riding a bare-backed horse. She was naked and wet from being in the canal. She was in possession of all her limbs and her breasts were just beginning to form. Weeks into pubescence and she didn't know, didn't yet realize that her days riding around naked on a horse were numbered. Alcohol burned an aperture behind his eyes and he felt a stirring in his body, the kind of stirring you do not want anyone else to see.

He looked at Denis crouching at his side and thought about the way he engineered violent situations in prison to deliver Harry, his best friend, from harm. Harry liked Denis. He just liked him. He had a spot in his heart for failures, for routine fuck-up artists like Denis. If Harry had any fault at all, it was the inclination to romanticize. He was sentimental about people stuck at the bottom of the social pile, who never understood what the current dispensation was offering, who could not rise up from their beds and go ride the New Wave. But not for one moment did Harry think this relationship with Denis symbiotic, while hoping his relationship with Gabrielle was. He felt immune only from failure, not from success.

'Did I ever tell you about my uncle's house on the canal?' Denis slurred. 'He owned a little lock cottage.'

'And now you have a little toilet on the same canal. How quaint.'

'Fuck off, Harry. I really liked that little house.'

'The Welsh call a little house and an outside toilet by the same name. They call it, Tŷ Bach.'

'I didn't know you were Welsh, Harry?'

'Why do you say that?'

'Since you can speak the language, I thought ...'

'Don't assume anything about me. Just because I can speak two words of Welsh doesn't mean I'm Welsh. I can speak three words of Spanish. When people think they know where you come from, they always think they know what kind of person you are. A lot of people don't like the Welsh. I don't like the Welsh. They're always up to no good.' In anger, Harry pushed Denis.

Denis disappeared under the surface of the canal. With a head swimming in alcohol, Harry was slow to react. He began shouting his name as though Denis could snatch at it like a rope. The seriousness of the situation began percolating through after Denis failed to reappear. Then Denis's curved back broke the surface. His back was followed by his shoulders and head as if he'd been touching his toes underwater. Denis had fallen in over a horse ramp where the water was only a few feet deep.

Denis reached out his hand to Harry. As soon as he beached himself, he began scrambling a monologue about his uncle's lock cottage. Since he'd pushed him into the canal, Harry felt obliged to indulge him.

'Whenever my old man used to knock me around I used to go there. I wished I could have lived in it with him. It was a little life-saver. I liked it even the first time I saw it. An old white cottage he'd paid fifteen thousand for. I bet it's worth a hundred and fifty thousand now, being on water. He was always doing something to make it better. It was bright white with a yellow door, then a red one, or blue. Every year he changed the colour. It had two bedrooms, sitting-room and kitchen and nicely decorated. He never had lace curtains on the windows. Boaters looked right inside at him eating breakfast. He made wine from the grapes growing in his garden and we'd sit on his doorstep in the summer, drinking the wine, talking and laughing with the boaters as they waited for the lock to fill up. They always had to squint up at the cottage because it was so bright.'

Harry teased the Yale into the top lock, suspecting there was someone already in as the Chubb had not been closed. Harry continued breaking and entering regardless, in a fighting kind of mood. The door gave silently and Gauloise cigarette smoke irritated his nostrils. Then he heard his name mentioned, but not in calling. Apparently he was being discussed. He stood in the doorway to the hall. Through the large bay window of the lounge he could see two pairs of feet jutting into the garden. Gabrielle and Samson were sitting on the steps leading to the garden from her kitchen, talking it over.

'Harry's sub-text, Peter. Not even that. Don't be suspicious.' Harry heard Gabrielle saying.

'What the fuck's sub-text?' Samson asked. Harry held his breath so as to hear the answer. He wanted to know also.

'Just a distraction. Christ, I'm meant to be in love with a petty criminal from Madrid every night in front of a thousand people. I didn't really know how to respond to this guy. Then Harry walks into the theatre. It was a gift. He's helped me raise my game.'

'Do you know he's going around London with your keys?'

'Is he!'

'He lets himself in when you're not here.'

Gabrielle snorted. 'The cheeky bastard. Well, I guess he's a thief, after all. A real one.'

'He could clean you out.'

'Harry's a pickpocket, not a burglar. People like him are such creatures of habit. He is no more likely to rob my hi-fi than become a social worker.'

'So there is nothing going on between you two?'

'Do me a favour, Peter.'

'If you're sleeping with the bloke I'd rather know than not know. I can put a contract out on him then.'

'Peter!'

'He's a good-looking guy …'

'So are you.'

'Yeah, except I haven't been around for a while.'

'I've been waiting for you, honey, you know that. You believe me, don't you?'

'I want to, darling. But it's a little hard when the day I walk out of court after being banged up twelve months, the first person I meet is not you, but Harry fucking Langland letting himself in like he lives here.'

'Every actress needs a mascot, Peter.' Gabrielle breathed on the words. 'Harry's my little mascot, for the duration of this play. Don't be jealous.'

The flat went silent. He could only suspect what she

was doing now to ratify her false statement. So many lies had left her mouth, so many truths concealed, Harry didn't know how he should feel. But since actors were in a permanent state of rehearsal, it was a piece of cake for them to weave out of trouble. And since he knew she was pregnant by a man unknown, Harry came down on the side that Gabrielle had spun Samson a good one. The opposite of what she had just said about Harry must have been true. He was more than a mascot, more than just a distraction. Still, it felt uncomfortable being a fly on the wall, like being at your own funeral. Harry was reminded of the time in his life when this had happened before. He had overheard his parents then, through a closed door, when he was seven. His mother and father were arguing bitterly, cooling down by agreeing that their problem was Harry. Their marriage had started falling apart after Harry arrived. It would have been better if their only child had never been born. They couldn't afford children. As soon as Harry was old enough to leave home, his father suggested, things would improve again. His mother screamed. She said she couldn't wait that long. Harry digested it all philosophically, as children do, when reacting to disaster.

'I'd drop him dead if I thought you were stepping out with him. I'll get the keys off him if you want me to. Do you want me to get the keys?'

'I can do that. If I enjoyed having men look after me, I'd be fucking policemen.'

'Okay, okay.' Samson laughed. The mood was relaxing on the kitchen steps. 'In a funny kind of way Harry reminds me of myself. I had nothing to start with, either. Just a sharp suit, like his. But please make sure you get your keys off him.'

Harry gently closed the door and backed out into the street. His first call was to a hardware store where he got another set of her keys cut.

ELEVEN

Regent's Canal between Angel and Limehouse was macabre in its dereliction. Where steel-mesh window-screens had rusted away or hung on one hinge, not a single piece of glass remained intact. Two small boys demolishing a wall with sledge-hammers hurled the shattered brick at wire-reinforced glass. Empty ware-house gave way to empty workshop: mute valedictions to a bygone age. Prefabricated buildings of a school on the opposite bank had been gutted by fire. Chairs, desks, blackboards violently ejected through smashed windows formed an island in the canal. The school was succeeded by a length of wall with no windows or orifices of any kind. Pipes jutting out of the sweatshops issued toxic blue smoke. Single light bulbs burned behind shuttered windows. Blackened wrought-iron fire-escapes hurried down from crumbling asbestos roofs.

Gabrielle had asked Harry to accompany her and Samson down this moribund stretch of canal. At first he didn't understand why she was interested in going. Perhaps such wastelands underlined her glittering success, reminded her that she had it all. Or it reflected the constructs of her own personality as an actor. Perhaps she thought it would be good for Samson, a walk along water designed to get his mind back on the job. Harry led them down the tow-path like a tourist guide.

A hot, sweet wind stroked their faces. The canal bank receded into open spaces with twelve-storey blocks of flats dumped in the grass like amputated stumps, their skin flaking away and piling up on the ground. Young children fought bitterly on top of chipboard and breeze block hills. It was the architecture of exhaustion. Harry was glad to be living aboard *Irish Jack*. Far better to wake up in the night and see the moon on the water than the floodlight-lashed flanks of such high-rise blocks. Historical graffiti – MATTHEWS FRAMED GEORGE DAVIS – were overlaid with the new: NO SUPER-GRASSES. SUPERGRASSES OUT, and competed for wall space with the myriad TV satellite dishes, bolted on like pale-grey fungi. One block looked phantom with all its windows broken and the entire third floor stoved in by a sawn-down oak tree.

Alongside Gabrielle and Samson, Harry felt vulnerable. This was outlaw country. He wasn't frightened for what they had in their pockets, more for their health. His charges were enriched in more ways than one, and they stood out against the fawn canal like Pacific blossom. They could easily become targets of folks round here, who, like dogs irritated by the heat, bite the nearest flesh. Spontaneous combustion was a term that came to mind. Ramblers of Gabrielle's and Samson's calibre got pushed in the water or stabbed without motive.

'Do people still live here? What kind of life goes on here? What *is* that smell?' Gabrielle was full of questions.

'People round here bite just because it's hot outside,' said Harry.

Samson had been very quiet the whole time. He had emptied a packet of boiled sweets into his suit jacket pocket and ate one after another. He broke his silence for the first time after he'd eaten them all. 'I like this canal, Harry. It's a lost piece of London.'

'Yeah, and look at the state it's in,' Gabrielle added. 'When was it built?'

'In the 1820s,' Harry estimated.

'I've never really noticed this end of the canal before. It's a good site. But it needs developing. These warehouses and stuff aren't ever going to be used again. It would be better to turn them round than have a strip of concrete running down here. If you developed a new system for going through the locks faster, people could commute to work on boats. It could be fantastic. I see derelict sites like these and get a vision of what they could be. Then I look at the site again as it is and start piecing the vision together. Property development's like a jigsaw.'

Samson unbuttoned his collar and slackened his tie. It was getting warmer and Harry felt tempted to do the same to his, but it would have looked to Gabrielle like he was under Samson's influence. 'Even as a kid I was always restoring things. I'd find a bike frame tossed in some blackberry brambles, then go around dumps getting wheels and things until I ended up with a whole bike. I am a romantic, really. I like to create something beautiful out of the ruins. It's not the money. I love the game.'

On the opposite side of the canal, development opportunity signs were ubiquitous, but they only saw one bonded warehouse that had actually been converted. All the new flats in this warehouse were empty except for one. Its French windows were flung wide open onto a balcony too small to take even a single chair. The balcony overhung an old loading bay in the canal which had become a depository for plastic bottles, shredded polystyrene and fly-tipped builders' rubble coated in pigeon shit. An estate agents' guinea-pig in a white bathrobe roamed around inside on bare polished floorboards, scratching his chin, wondering whether he could leave off shaving for another day.

Samson stopped to look deeply into the warehouse. 'So there *is* a precedent here. Someone's turning them around. And one guy's in. That's enough to bring in the others.'

They walked on to Limehouse basin, where the canal poured into the Thames. The river was very busy on a flood tide. A ballast dredger was entering an aggregate base, churning water as it backed-up in mid-stream. Samson started up again. 'There is too much optimism among developers. They think they can sell anything. But boomtimes end. Someday this boomtime will end. It's better to have no growth or small growth because building takes a long time. I'm pretty reckless about that myself. I'll turn something around in nine months by paying men double to work around the clock seven days a week. London Docklands is going to fail because it's taking too long. The bottom of the property market is going to fall through before they finish and then they won't be able to shift anything.'

Port of London divers were working off a driftwood barge, a kind of Hoover on the water, anchored off the north wall. Harry wondered if they had found another leg. With so many limbs missing, that corpse would be an amphibious sort of thing now, travelling down the river to the sea and the origins of species.

'You know why I've had so much success developing waterside property?' Samson asked, to set himself up with the answer. 'Because water symbolizes a mother's affection.'

'And we all need that when we're ill,' Harry added swiftly.

'That's right,' Samson smiled.

'Swinburne called the sea "a great sweet mother",' Gabrielle said distantly, coldly, as though disapproving.

'Who's Swinburne?' Samson asked, suspiciously. 'Do I know him?'

'I doubt it. He died in 1909.'

'We are all born in water,' Samson continued.

'I still don't get the connection to property development,' Gabrielle said.

'What I'm saying is, we were born in water. Amniotic fluid. Before that, long before, we came from the sea. We emerge from water and spend the rest of our lives worrying and fretting about the purpose of life, don't we? But whenever you house people next to water, they instantly find a profound peace, like they've come home. It's the primeval instinct that I satisfy.'

A tug passed upstream, towing a brace of 100-foot litter barges. Lightermen strolled along gunwales, waving fraternally to the divers on the driftwood barge feeding out airlines to their colleagues below. 'Lightermen have worked this river for a thousand years,' Samson said.

'What's a lighterman?' Gabrielle asked, looking at the river, its details escaping her. The Thames was just a brackish wedge that flowed through her life in an accidental way.

Gabrielle receded in Harry's mind's eye, and possibly in Samson's too, as they swapped their knowledge of the river. 'Lightermen see London beyond the river banks as a foreign land,' Harry remarked. 'Most of them can't even drive cars.'

He and Samson stared across the river to the south shore, discussing the rivalry that existed between lightermen's communities north and south of the river; a rivalry between Catholics and Protestants. 'Lightermen were northsiders and southsiders according to religion, but on the river they were onesiders, because they had one common enemy. That water. One day they may have to pull each other out.'

Harry watched the lightermen walk on water and felt his heart tugged. 'The river gives them life.'

'In a life-threatening occupation ...'

'You two know a lot about waterways,' Gabrielle suddenly broke in, determined not to be upstaged. She had had enough of being on the periphery. She had been quiet for too long. 'I never regarded acting to be a life-threatening occupation until someone vowed to kill me on stage.' She turned her back to the Thames, taking over the story.

'When was this?'

'I was in *Macbeth* at Stratford and some bastard wrote to me saying he'd set light to my car the night he was planning to kill me.'

'That's nice. What happened?' Harry asked.

'He set light to my car.'

'Well, you're still here,' chimed Samson. 'I guess he failed.'

'I was in my dressing-room when security came in and told me they had just put out a fire underneath my Audi. The curtain had already gone up, Macbeth was on with the witches, and I thought, ah well, fuck it, let it all come down. In for a penny, in for a pound.

'You can't see much of the audience from the stage. They're like shadows, you know? I went on and played the Lady to an imagined face of my dear assassin. I played it with *insane* energy. It was the best performance I've ever given. I put the whole theatre through the wringer, including the cast.'

'But nothing happened?'

'I reached my final line "To bed, to bed …" and knew I'd made it through the night. The worst part was having to go down to the police station to make a statement. The detective sergeant took one look at me, at the stage make-up caked on my face, and suggested I might have provoked the threat. As though being an actress was the same as being a bloody whore. He was a real cunt.' Gabrielle kicked a stone. 'The police are cowards, bloody imbeciles!'

'Hear, hear,' said Harry.

'We all agree on that, then.' Samson and Harry laughed together. The two men were now on back-slapping terms. This did not go unnoticed by Gabrielle.

'You two *buddies* want to stop for a bout of arm wrestling?' She stalked away from them, raising an imaginary shotgun to a family of ducks on the water. Her green and blue eyes burned holes in the monochrome landscape, minute by minute transforming herself into a woman Harry didn't know.

The lightermen on the litter barges went out of sight. A pleasure boat passed down to Greenwich. People danced on the decks to rock music, tipped wine into the river, waved indiscriminately at everybody. Harry waved back for good luck. They were more his industry than lightermen in the end. The tourists.

They went down to the Thames so Samson could read

a timetable for boats to Greenwich. They would have to wait an hour as the next boat in was already full. The queue was lining up on the pier. Quickly, Harry linked his arms inside Samson's and Gabrielle's. He was painfully excited. 'Don't look now, but there's a dipper working this queue. He's on our left. If you look too closely he'll see you and then he'll be off. He's wearing a flat cap and a brown raincoat. There's a rolled-up newspaper in his hand. He looks part of the queue, except he's holding back a bit, his eyes are darting a bit, all on one level.'

'I see him. I see him!' Gabrielle hissed through her lips.

'Where?' Samson's eyes were turning in his head.

'Next to the woman with the three kids.'

'Good God. He just put his hand into that woman's bag.'

Harry retrieved his arms, glad to have shown off his ability to see below the surface. Samson slapped him on the back. They cantered up to the canal again, three thoroughbred fans of deception.

An hour later they called in for a drink at a canalside pub. Harry had suggested they go to a five-star restaurant, thinking they would prefer it, but Gabrielle dismissed that idea and chose the Duke of Sussex over the Sir Walter Scott, filled with men who looked as though they'd been in a session all day. Gabrielle and Harry sat down while Samson went to the bar. He ordered three large Irish whiskeys and three pints of Guinness to chase. He brought the whiskeys over to the table and went back to wait for the stout to be poured. As he was moving through the crowd, Gabrielle twisted herself around to look Harry squarely in the face. 'Harry, do you think you could return my flat keys you borrowed? In your own time, of course.'

Harry, prepared for this question since overhearing their conversation, casually forked out three keys on a ring and handed them in. 'Sorry,' he said, coolly.

She pulled Harry's face towards her and kissed him fully on the mouth, scouring the insides of his cheeks with her tongue.

Harry ducked, in anticipation of a blow from Samson. But he was still busy at the bar. Harry was ecstatic. That kiss was an index of her commitment. It was all he needed to feel hope for their future, a future that must have felt stronger than the one Samson was facing.

When Samson arrived with the Guinness, Harry was full of crazy laughter and of Burgess's voice in his head, mourning the lack of friends in her life. *'I used to have a lot of friends but they were all so sick in one way or the other. A bad lot. Having no friends is better than that.'*

'I'm your friend,' Harry shouted. 'I'm your best fucking friend.'

'Good,' said Samson. 'We like you too.'

'I had a vision the other night,' Burgess was saying to him. 'We were on the boat together, you, me, Simmy. She was sitting up in her cot watching me varnish the floor. You were reclining in the bosun's cabin, hands behind your head. The boat was completely fitted out, tied up against a leafy bank somewhere out of London. There was this easy silence hanging between us, down the entire length of the boat, like we'd been together for years.'

Her vision troubled Harry. It did not fit into his scheme of things. He had a new girlfriend in the Successful Tradition; a woman he thought he'd lost before her kiss in the pub. In the end, he preferred women with jewellery rather than purple cicatrices.

'Look, Burgess, I've got plans. I mean …' He stopped to mull this over. Maybe he was unnecessarily limiting his options. Burgess and Gabrielle hardly moved in the same circles; there was little chance of them meeting up. He saw no harm in a little make-believe and encouraged Burgess's aspirations for the moment, telling her how good it was to touch her, the only woman in his life. 'I want to do right by you, Burgess.' Harry sealed his promise with a kiss.

Burgess stretched out on the floor and dozed off. Harry tried to nap but he was too aroused by her body. The winos outside were mumbling low, furrowed ballads, which covered Harry, stealthily lifting Burgess's nightshirt from behind. He dipped her salty nexus, still believing that taking something away from a woman without bothering her was an act of chivalry. She was very wet inside. Perhaps she was dreaming of this, he thought.

Burgess woke up with a scream, so loud the men stopped singing instantly. Harry reversed out and was caught red-handed. Her rough, work-worn fingers clamped around his penis. Then he started shouting. The boat rocked suddenly with bodies jumping on the sides, their voices clamouring in the dark. The door was kicked open. 'Burgess? Burgess?'

'It's okay,' she placated them. 'I was having a nightmare.' When they had retreated she reproached Harry: 'So that's how a pickpocket makes love, is it?'

TWELVE

Since Peter Samson had been out on bail, his old friends and colleagues had not returned his phone calls. Harry was the only man he could talk to. Harry listened like he always did, with consummate skill. Samson hated solitude. He needed to tell boastful stories about himself, repeating several of them more than once. When Harry asked to see some of his work, Samson arranged for a limousine to pick them up from Gabrielle's and take them to one of his sites, where the Grand Union Canal and the Thames meet at Brentford.

At the junction of Augustus Close and Brent Way, twenty-six flats surrounded a spectacular landscaped garden on a gradient to the canal. Seven years ago he stumbled on this place when it had been a block of tatty shops with residential space above. He had a vision, inspired by their art deco features and the water, of how he could develop them. The local environment had selling potential. Syon Park was close, Kew Gardens directly across the river. Syon Gardens had a butterfly farm and fabulous walks to the Thames. At nearby Brentford docks was a sailing club. Rail, road and river intersected there, making commuting easy. It was a gift, a great place to live if only there were units to live in. Samson decided he wanted to own the whole block with all its land.

One of the buildings was for sale, a paint store on the corner of the block. Samson bought this and dug in. Behind the store was a Nissen hut, blocking access to the rear of the other three buildings. Samson found who the owner was and offered to buy it. The next day the owner arrived in a 1961 Bentley. The first thing he told Samson was how much he had hated his father. The only thing he had given his son was this Nissen hut, with a brief to make his fortune off it. The hut was all he was getting by way of a start, a damn sight more than he had started out with. His son rented it out, first to a chandler, then a boat builder, using the rent to finance a laundry empire. The old man was dead now, but his son wanted to keep the hut as a memorial to his father's meanness. It had sentimental value. Harry showed him the corrosion on the hut. It wasn't going to last very long unless someone took it over. If he let Samson buy it, he would keep it renovated. And he could come around to see it whenever he liked. The day after Samson signed the papers, he tore down the hut.

Beside the paint store was a recently rebuilt shop. The land at the back was empty, overgrown with nettles and brambles. The freeholder leased out the shop to a camping equipment seller. The freeholder only knew what the land was worth organically, not in the context of Samson's vision. Samson made him an offer. When the freeholder started looking 'constipated', Samson offered him a little more. 'But that's my top offer. Take it or leave it.' The owner took the offer. 'In terms of what I had in mind, it was worth ten times that. But I kept my thoughts to myself,' he told Harry.

The owner of the third building was planning to turn his shop into an amusement arcade. In order to get a licence he had to have rear access to the building to meet with fire regulations. But now Samson owned the land behind two of the buildings and blocked his access. He played his trump card and made a deal: if he bought the building off him in exchange for access, he would lease the shop back to him. Samson let him go down the road with his plan for an amusement arcade, without intending to renew his lease after the first term.

An old man owned the last building with an outhouse in the rear. He renovated furniture in the outhouse and sold the pieces in the shop. Samson told the guy his furniture was becoming dated and would soon be hard to sell. But the old man liked his work. The stock of furniture constituted many years' collecting. Since he was interested in the stock and not the building, Samson set fire to the outhouse with all its furniture. The old man claimed on the insurance and Samson bought the buildings and the land off the insurance company.

Now Samson owned all the buildings and all the land. Since the buildings were so attractive with their art deco features, he decided to try to get them listed. 'You can claim VAT refunds on materials used for renovating listed buildings, bugger all if they're not. My architect told me English Heritage would turn the application down because the shop fronts had been replaced. I found photographs of the brass inlaid originals and had replicas built on the quiet. Then I went to English Heritage and they listed them. Simple people in the Heritage. I saved eighty thou that way on VAT alone. Just a little anecdote for you, Harry. They've all been sold now, or I'd give you one. Since you like the canal so much.'

'I live on the canal, actually on the water.' Harry thought about whether to make the next confession or not, then decided it would help cement things, since it was a man-to-man talk. 'I live on a boat. An expensive flat's a waste of capital to my mind. All I want is a place to put my head down, you know what I mean? I'm not a homemaker.'

As they walked to the car, a twelve-year-old girl in a French plait cried out euphorically as they passed her by. She bent down and retrieved a diamond lizard brooch someone had dropped. She squinted and turned it in her hand to catch the light. 'See!' – Samson nudged Harry – 'this place is full of treasure waiting to be found.'

Samson owned many properties, but his principal address, as submitted to Harry, was a bedsit in Shoreditch. It was to this attic room in a Victorian house that they next journeyed in the limo. He claimed to spend one night a month there for sentimental reasons. This had been his first home, fifteen years ago. When he became wealthy, he bought the whole house off his former landlord and left it as it was.

He showed Harry around the place. The only personal item he kept in his room was a 9mm bullet he had fired through his own hand as a kid. Surreptitiously Harry looked for a scar but saw nothing. The bed and armchair belonged to the old landlord and smelled of domestic animals. 'My first home, Harry. A piece of shit. I keep it to remind myself of the advances I've made. It's a good luck thing. I also pay for a little pussy once in a while and bring it here. But don't tell Gabrielle that.'

Gabrielle might be relieved to know. Harry stored it away to use as a weapon if necessary. It was the first of many revelations Samson was to make to him.

There were three other bedsits in the house, although he rarely met his tenants. He only knew who they were from their mail, which he habitually opened: a Nigerian single mother, an unemployed Irish couple and a schizophrenic evicted from Friern Barnet hospital. He heard their lives bumping and colliding below the floor and through the walls. 'They may have been switched by now, since I've been inside. I've got an agent who rents all the rooms except for this one. This stays empty for me. I keep the rent very low. It's the same as what I paid when I lived here, fifteen years ago. You can use this place whenever you like, Harry. Bring some pussy over.' Samson chuckled and threw him the keys.

Yeah, like Gabrielle, Harry thought.

In summer Samson's building was a tree house. Branches of lime trees fingered his window and for half the year their leaves blotted out his view of the city. He had preferred it that way. Sometimes it was best to have no view at all: the trees concealed a women's prison below.

'I read somewhere that for every one woman in prison there are twenty-seven men,' Samson began, leaning out of the window. 'Women aren't drawn to crime like men. If crime enhances masculinity, it has a wrinkling effect on femininity. I told Gabby that and you know what she said? Women like to fuck a man's career and, for her money, criminals have the biggest balls of all.' Samson laughed. 'Isn't she a piece of work, Harry?'

Harry tried reversing Samson's theory in his mind: imagining himself as the actor and Gabrielle as the thief, and he did not like the concept. Of all women in prison, the majority were prostitutes and, unlike Samson, Harry had never once gone with one of those.

Whenever Samson got too ambitious in his work, he would go to the bedsit and take a long hard stare at the prison through the foliage. The sight of inmates' underwear drying in the sun was his deterrent against imprudence. 'When I was renting this room I was on the dole. I had twenty-two pounds a week to live on and I thought fuck this, I can't live like this. An old friend of mine, who I went to school with, was doing out property in Islington, before Islington got expensive. He gave me a piece of advice and a false reference. I took his reference to the bank and got a loan to buy my first property. It was an old Methodist chapel around the corner from here. It was a listed building and I got it for nothing, because no one else wanted it. To renovate the chapel would have cost a fortune. To knock it down and build on the site was the only way to make a good return, but you can't knock down listed buildings, unless they are structurally unsound. The next thing I did was drive up to North Wales and talk to a man who worked in a slate quarry. I made this deal with him. For a couple of thousand pounds he stole some dynamite from the quarry and came back to London with me. We sank the dynamite into the foundations and exploded it. As soon as the dust cleared we found cracks in the wall. I got a structural report done and that was that. It said the building was dangerous. So I got permission to knock it down. Now there's fourteen flats there, all sold.'

Harry wondered why he never told stories like this. Probably he felt guilty about what he did. Samson wasn't bothered by ethics at all. He was like a boy in many ways, bragging about his pranks. It kept a sparkle in his eye.

'When you work like I do, in billions of pounds, you make a lot of hard enemies. I mean people who would kill you, given the chance. Before the shit hit the fan, I could protect myself. But now I feel pretty damn vulnerable. Like exposed. It's a miserable feeling to hear that some people are out looking for me. You know what I mean, Harry? You must run the gauntlet a bit, in your business?'

'Yeah, with fences. Bastards would chop your fingers off for the sake of loose change.'

'I can't stay with Gabrielle while all this is going on. Too dangerous for her. And I can't stay at Mayfair, or my place in the country. I can't even stay here. Everyone I don't want to know knows about these places. I'm a bloody outlaw.'

'Where will you stay?'

'You haven't got a spare bed, I suppose?'

'What, on the boat?' Harry was taken by surprise. His initial response to try to put Samson off was tempered by a sudden shaft of foresight. Peter Samson was asking for his help. A millionaire. Something good had to come out of that. Then he got real. Burgess owned the boat, which was a floating slum anyway, under a crumbling construction site. 'The boat is in a bit of a mess. I mean you're welcome, but you'd have to sleep on piles of timber. There's no bath installed yet.'

'Doesn't matter to me.'

Harry couldn't put him off. 'I'll have to square it with my builder. I'm paying a woman to do the work on it and she lives on the boat while it's going on. She's sensitive about strangers. It'll be all right, I'll just have to have a word.'

'You've got a woman living with you, Harry? You rascal. I was beginning to think you were queer.'

While it was prudent to have Samson thinking he was balling someone other than Gabrielle, he didn't want the news travelling to Gabrielle. 'It's nothing like that,' he decided. 'I employ her. She's got a baby to feed. She needs the money.'

'A charitable pickpocket. Well, that's interesting, Harry. I belong to the Variety Club. Charity's good for the soul. Good for the image, too.' Samson took the keys from Harry to lock up the bedsit, then gave them back. 'Be sure to use the place now.'

They wandered along the tow-path of the canal towards Marylebone, so Harry could show him the narrow boat. He kept warning Samson that it wasn't much to look at and about the construction site above. But Samson said he didn't mind how rough it was, as long as it was safe. 'The more obscure, the safer it's likely to be.'

They were both dressed in blue suits, not identical blues but which gave off the same message nevertheless. The wind kept blowing Samson's grey fringe of hair into his face, which he dragged out of his eyes, as Gabrielle was inclined to do, with a fast sweep of his open hand. 'Whenever I'm near a strip of water it just makes me want to travel,' said Samson.

'What are you going to do, like after the trial?' Harry asked.

'If I live that long, you mean? Between you and me, I don't think I'm going to get off. I'm expecting to go down on this one. I can't face five years' prison, Harry. What would you do, in my position?'

'I'd go to Europe, I think. It's all meant to be happening there.'

Samson chewed gum as he walked. 'Say I skip bail,' he said suddenly. 'Go to Europe. I could re-invent myself, like an actor. Get a new role. A new identity.' He stretched out his arms as though on a cross. 'I could be someone else. I've done it before. I'd rather be someone else than dead, or a nobody rotting in a prison cell. Life's too short to die young, or lose five years. At the moment I have to check in at the police station once a week. They've taken my passport.' His face dropped.

'Don't you know anyone with a boat? You could go beach to beach from here to France.'

'I do know someone, actually. The guy who gave me that dodgy reference. Eddie. Fuck, I wonder if I can still find him ...' He took out a new pack of gum and offered one to Harry.

The speed his plans were developing made Harry giddy. He had never thought so fast or so far, working on his own contingency plans. With Samson out of the way, he and Gabrielle could be at it again. Harry encouraged him fiercely.

A barge heading the same direction caught up with them on the tow-path. Burgess was at the tiller with Simmy strapped to her cot on the roof. Harry waved her down and she threw him her stern line. He coiled the rope around his arm and brought the boat to a standstill against the bank. Samson, propped up against a wall, was so lost in thought he hadn't even realized what was happening. 'This is my boat I was telling you about,' Harry said. 'Hop aboard.'

Samson jumped tentatively on the front deck. A smell of hot sweet oil issued from inside the cabin. Harry raised his hand over the cabin roof to Burgess who drove the engine up an octave. Thick smoke issued from the chimney as the boat pushed away from the wall back into the centre of the canal.

The water ahead was glassy, sucking bridges, trees

and sky under its surface. The bow cut this scaled-down picture-globe like scissors, silently and unswervingly. It was more like gliding, Harry thought, his racing mind dissolving into the water like salt. They passed between factory walls that contained the water in a private world, which for the moment belonged to Harry and Samson alone.

Going through Islington tunnel, Harry felt like an aviator navigating through a night sky. The tunnel aperture was reduced to a point of brilliancy like the moon. Water dripped from the roof onto his wrists. The air was black and curious in the ellipsis. The engine droning seventy feet away was hardly audible.

'There is something very primeval about tunnels,' Samson whispered in the darkness.

The canal continued to climb after they left the tunnel. Harry worked with Burgess in the locks while Samson sat being creative on the bow deck, pensively re-inventing the waterborne landscape and himself in it.

Aside, he asked Burgess if she minded Samson staying for a few nights.

'Who is he?'

'He's a property developer.'

'A property developer with nowhere to live?'

'His wife's thrown him out. It's just while he gets back on his feet.'

'You have to stay too.'

'Of course. Unless I've got something on.'

'No, Harry. If he's going to stay, then I want you to stay too.'

'What about Irish Jack and the boys? You don't need me. They look after you pretty well. Anyway, Peter's a gentleman.'

'Gentlemen are the worst. Charm kills, don't you know?'

Locking-up, Harry tied the bow line to a ring and opened the ground paddle with the windlass on the same side, creating a circulation of water that held the boat tight on the bow line and hard against the side of the lock chamber. Once the chamber had flooded he leant on the balance beam to open the top gates, feeling his body's pleasure. He closed all paddles behind them on leaving each lock, carefully winding them down on the rack.

Burgess was heading back to Marylebone, now that she had exercised the boat. As they cut into the basin under the transitory landscape of cranes and scaffolding, Samson gave out a sigh. These were the tools of his trade. A development site was another of his spiritual homes.

After they had tied up under the ice warehouse, Harry and Samson sat on foam rubber, while Burgess kept a little distance further down the boat. She didn't trust strangers and this one was potentially as bad as the rest. 'Who is she, anyway?' Samson whispered. 'A mermaid?'

Irish Jack lay on the cobblestones outside, drunk on duty. He ran a cold stare down Samson's spine when they arrived, but let him off, being in Harry's custody.

Harry asked Samson a question he'd been meaning to ask for a long time. He felt close enough to the man now to raise it. 'What did you do, Peter, to get into trouble? Did you blow something up?'

'Nothing like that.' He paused. For a moment Harry thought that was all he would get. It seemed to cost Samson just to be reminded of it. 'No, nothing got blown up. I had just acquired all that property at Brentford we've just seen and was ready to build. I applied for planning permission to the council and the British Waterways Board. The housing and planning committee go out inspecting these sites on coaches. After inspecting a site they go back to the coach and discuss the applications. After they inspected my site I gatecrashed their meeting on the coach. I promoted a discussion. I asked them if they'd be giving me planning permission. The majority said they saw no reason why not. So I left the coach and switched off the tape.'

'What tape?'

'I went on wired for sound.'

'Why?'

'I'll tell you now. After a month I heard that they'd turned down my application so I took the tape in and played it back. I accused them of taking a bribe from someone else who'd put in a tender. They began to shit themselves. If it wasn't true this time, it was true for others. I *know*. I've bribed them myself. They told me the property assets sub-committee chairman of the Waterways Board had opposed the application. Whenever I think about him now I feel like I'm drowning. His name sounded like someone gargling water: Domino Waunarlydd. Before he joined the BWB he used to run Elsdale floating school at Little Venice. This Waunarlydd character was opposed to my plans. He wanted the area developed as part of a limited water transportation scheme. It made all the right noises ecologically. It was going to create hundreds of jobs. But it was a dream. Old Waunarlydd was sixty years old. He was a raving Baptist. He never got married, or had any children. The waterway was his family. But what he also did was a bit of teaching, local waterways history in the evenings to top up his income. So I joined his class in an adult education centre. After class I'd take him to the pub and pump him all night about the place at Brentford. I was trying to turn him around to my way of thinking. One night he took me to the canal at Norwood to try and *show* me how he felt. We stood in the BWB maintenance yard, overlooking the eleven-lock drop to the river, and he described how the canal used to be when he first came to London. He waxed on about how it was crammed with boats loading and unloading coal, sand, gravel, timber, the tow-path full of horses and drays. 'You could walk across the canal on barges,' he'd say. 'Now every day is like a Sunday.' After a whole year taking his class, I gave up. He wouldn't let go of the past. So I had him topped. We made him disappear, Harry, into the River Brent, and I assumed the problem was solved. But instead of going down with the Thames, old Waunarlydd floated back into the fucking canal.'

Burgess had been standing at the nearest bulkhead trying to get Simmy to sleep over her shoulder. She had heard everything. Her face was serious and wan as she came in.

'Water has a memory,' she warned Samson.

THIRTEEN

Harry was weaving in and out of the station concourse, visiting the ticket office, bookstore and coffee shop. Every woman he tried to tap sprang to life the moment she came within the circle of his influence. He squandered some time among them in grand fantasy as surfer, seaman, salamander before giving up on himself to join Samson and Gabrielle at the pond on Hampstead Heath.

Harry walked along the jetty, sucking in his paunch, one step behind Samson. Harry had the palest skin of the three. His shoulders were not as wide as Samson's either, and his legs were thinner. Samson looked quite athletic. He must have worked out in gaol.

Gabrielle wanted to swim out to the raft anchored in the middle of the pond where half a dozen swimmers lay sunbathing. She jumped and screamed against the chill as she hit the water. Harry gave Samson a massive push in the back, then dived in and swam underwater in pitch darkness with his eyes open until his lungs gave out. He surfaced, vigorously ploughing a trough through the brown water. His desire to beat Samson to the raft was a huge obsessive need pressing against his chest. Winning that race was the only thing that mattered in the world. The water sparkled around his face as he kicked his legs furiously, shaking off the feel of some underwater creature pulling him down.

He looked back to see how Samson was progressing, expecting him to be steaming along. Samson was in fact struggling to keep his head out of the water, in the same place he had entered, with Harry's help, six feet out from the jetty. Harry stopped swimming. He turned around and carved back to Samson with a huge slicing stroke. He scooped his arms under Samson's armpits and then dragged him backwards to a buoy a few metres away. Harry introduced Samson to the buoy, and he clung on like a possessive child. He was panting and gasping and belched a couple of times.

'Jesus Christ, I'm sorry,' said Harry. 'I didn't know you couldn't swim.'

'I was just going to dangle my feet in the bloody water, Harry. Until you pushed me in.'

'How come you can't swim?' It seemed incongruous somehow, that a man who'd made millions from erecting real estate with an aqueous theme couldn't swim. Harry always found it odd when a man or a woman confessed they didn't know how. It was as shocking as if they couldn't talk.

Harry tried coaching Samson to the raft.

'No ... no ...'

'Nice and slowly. Come on. It's lovely out there.'

'Don't let me go. Don't fucking let me go.'

'I won't.'

They went from buoy to buoy. Samson struggled against Harry as though trying to fight him off. Harry swallowed a lot of the brown murky water and probably a few flies. He did contemplate letting Samson go, just to experience imaginatively the sense of power invested in him. He lay on his back for the final haul to the raft, with Samson between his legs. Harry held him under the chin and propelled with his free arm. He felt omnipotent, with Samson in this position, as if he had given birth to him.

He placed Samson's hand on the corner of the raft. Gabrielle had approached the raft by leisurely breast-stroke, keeping her hair dry. Now she sat with her legs in the water, looking down at Harry, the strong one, and Samson who felt so abjectly vulnerable he refused to catch her eye. Harry shot out of the pond and landed next to her, the water running off his pale torso. A handsome, boyish grin stretched over his blemish-free face. He breathed deeply and then he was still. Such a pretty boy, Harry, happy and, for the moment, blame-less. He let Samson fret for a few seconds, enjoying the aching dependency in his eyes for as long as possible.

Harry helped Samson onto the raft, where he expelled a lot of hot air before turning on his back. They sat in a row, Harry in the middle, flanked by several strangers with their faces up to the sky. The sun began to suck the moisture off their backs.

In a comfortable, tired silence they watched a man on the jetty climb a diving-board. He walked to the end, wiping his body on a chamois leather. He dropped the chamois to his feet, turned his back to the water and inched his heels over the edge, transformed into a statue, bronzed, glossy, motionless, before erupting into a pike dive, his face flat against his shins, snapping straight fifteen feet above the water. He parked in mid-air for a second before making his descent to part the water like a pair of curtains. A white two-seater aircraft cut its engines and slid through a cloudless blue sky above their heads.

This life was good. Life that began on the flesh and

worked outwards. There was nothing around that Harry could see likely to push things out of shape too fast. He forgot about the day-to-day problems of metropolitan life, forgot about the money he wasn't making and relaxed, massaged by the warm air.

But it didn't last long. He kept spinning away into uneasy conjecture. Fears and doubts of a totally abstract nature crashed into one another in his head like a motorway pile-up. He had no control over them. Somehow the pond itself was to blame. A pond was not as therapeutic as the canal, the river or the sea. The pond did not have an escape route, went nowhere; it had no horizons. You couldn't take a journey, real or imaginary, on a pond. The rim of the lake was like a fence that seemed to tighten around him. The people to get most out of it were treading water around the raft, discussing career moves – from civil law to conveyancing, from television into film production. The World is a pool to such people, into which you dive and make your short distance any which way you prefer.

Another diver climbed the ladder, fat and bald with a large gut hanging over his thong. He ran down the spring-board and launched himself off the end, his arms flailing and legs split apart. The water cracked like a whip and swallowed him.

Samson was still laughing a minute later when the wash rocked the raft. You try and do better, Harry wanted to say.

Gabrielle had on a black one-piece swimsuit. Clusters of short pubic hair sprang out the sides like iron filings. Her brown legs bent at right angles at the knee and disappeared into the water. Every few seconds her head would drop and she would fall asleep for an instant.

Three months pregnant and she was working harder than ever, sleeping less, eating hardly at all, as though the length of incubation was negotiable.

Samson gave Harry a wink to show that he knew Gabrielle wasn't quite with them, then whispered, 'Gabrielle told me the other day how you two met. When did you start boxing?'

Harry had a race on his hands trying to understand why Gabrielle would invent this, then remembered the adrenalin and gauze he'd taken to the theatre for her nosebleed. 'Ah, when I was fifteen, I guess ...'

Samson said he liked boxing, bantam weights being his favourite, so light they resembled ballet dancers who could still look pretty after a ten-year career. He said boxing was a silent theatre of tragedy, and he admired boxers for their research into their opponents. Harry relegated all his thoughts to memory, fully intending to pass them on to Gabrielle as his own insights.

They swam back together, with Samson like their child in the middle.

On the grass bank they lay in the sun. The small lawn was crammed with bodies, towels overlapping. People were talking, sunbathing, reading novels with utmost discretion. Ghetto blasters, ghetto folk found no way in. This was polite society and Gabrielle immediately found a role for Harry to play.

She lowered herself off her elbows and lowered her voice. 'There's a guy over there who I've been dying to work with all my life.' Harry and Samson were guided by her finger to the man in question. A gay bald aesthete in black Speedos and pince-nez glasses sat on a towel, drawing out manuscript pages from a leather briefcase like a conjuror. Gabrielle knew his CV inside out, all the films, opera and theatre he'd directed. 'I wonder what he's doing next. I bet that's the script.'

Samson was distracted by the trees that surrounded them, looking for gaps in the foliage, loopholes in the property law.

The director removed his glasses and dropped them into his briefcase, then went for a swim. Gabrielle squeezed Harry's bicep. 'Get me his briefcase, Harry …'

'What?'

'Get me his briefcase. Bring it over here.'

'Like, steal it?'

'Just for a second, then you can take it back.'

Harry looked around. There was no cover for such a job. She was asking a great deal. She saw Harry hesitate, noted Samson being distracted, then rolled down the top of her costume and bared her breasts to Harry. 'Pretty please,' she mouthed.

Harry was on his feet clutching a towel. He walked over to the briefcase and dropped his towel on it. He sat down next to it, waited a few seconds, then stood with the case inside the towel.

Gabrielle rifled through the contents, forcing sweat out on Harry's eyebrows. The name of the author on the script seemed to excite her. 'That's all I need to know.' Digging deeper still, she found several sheets of A4 paper stapled together, with names of actors on each sheet. 'These are the casting director's recommendations of who the script should be sent to.' She found a pen in the briefcase and scratched out the name on the top of the list and boldly printed her own name and agent alongside. 'That should do the trick.' Hurriedly she put the papers back in the case and snapped it shut. 'Now take it back,' she said.

Harry returned the briefcase in the same way as he had removed it, then walked back to Gabrielle to find her celebrating her act of stealth with Samson in her arms.

Gabrielle fell asleep for an hour between the two of them, her head slightly closer to Harry's elbow, he noticed, than to Samson's. When she woke, she sat bolt upright as if a cocked rifle were pressed against her temple. She remembered she had a show that evening. 'God, how could I forget! Can you imagine if I didn't turn up?' She noticed the director putting on his clothes to leave. 'I bet he's going off to canvass for the WRP. I should be more involved in the General Election somehow ...'

'General Election my ass,' Samson voiced. 'No one is interested in politics any more.'

Harry and Samson packed Gabrielle off in a taxi outside the park. 'Do you think she's going to be okay?' Harry asked, the warm air blowing through his hair.

'Nothing quite wakes you up like a live audience,' Samson reassured him.

She hardly seemed to recognize the two men waving her away on the pavement. She looked at them through the rear window with glazed eyes, her hair still wet. With the taxi out of sight, Harry and Samson were next to part company. Samson shook Harry's hand and said he was going out of town for a few days, to chase up some contacts.

FOURTEEN

Gabrielle strolled around the communal gardens, hand in hand with Samson, his hair tied back in a pony-tail. They stopped regularly to embrace and for him to whisper in her ear. They were plotting against Harry, who stood watching from the French windows. She was nine months pregnant; her maternity dress hung off her shoulders like a tent. A lot of people came into the garden just to watch them and so they wandered back into the flat, past Harry at the French windows, ignoring him completely. They entered the bedroom where Harry saw Samson rest his hands on her swollen belly.

Harry was awoken from this nightmare by Gabrielle's high laugh. She was sprawled naked on the bed, her belly flat as an ironing-board, trimming her pubic hair with the kitchen scissors. The telephone receiver was wedged between her shoulder and ear. The tone of her voice changed so dramatically seeing Harry wake that it made him wonder who she was talking to. He shook the vestiges of nightmare out of his skull and she covered her nakedness with a bathrobe, smiling at him but with another expression concealed underneath.

Someone in the flat above was playing *Tosca*, or so Gabrielle informed him the moment she hung up the phone. This was a measure of her culture that she could pin down an opera like that. Then the telephone rang again and this time she disappeared with the cordless receiver into the bathroom.

Harry padded into the kitchen in his boxer shorts. Gabrielle thought it an odd habit that he went to bed wearing underwear, but clothes meant a great deal more to him than to her. He couldn't bear to see himself naked, stripped of all illusions. He ground some espresso beans and packed the coffee into the metal pot as he had seen her do. He returned to the bedroom to get dressed.

He switched off the gas as the pot began to gurgle, poured a mug and took it in to her. She sat on the toilet, loosening the bathrobe around her waist, chatting in French into the telephone, waiting for the bath to fill. She laughed heavily and her breasts tumbled out of the gap in the robe.

He placed her coffee on the rim of the bath. Gabrielle stood and shook the robe off her shoulders. He watched it drop to her feet. She was performing a telephone striptease with the receiver in one hand. Now he was very curious about who she was talking to. Harry didn't like it when she spoke a foreign language. It excluded him, emphasized the social gap between them. He leaned against the shower door, watching her ease herself into the bath-water. When she could no longer ignore his presence in favour of someone else's, she cupped a hand over the mouthpiece and told him to go. 'I'm trying to have a conversation.'

'That's all right. Go ahead.'

'It's private.'

'It's French. I can't understand it, anyway.'

'Harry, don't be a jerk.' She turned on her stomach in the bath, her back to him.

'Don't turn your back on me. I said, don't turn your back on me.' Harry sensed himself being unmanned. He could not just walk away, not now. He had to recover that lost ground. Removing his clothes but keeping on his underpants, he stepped into the bath with an eye to forcing himself on her, to hose down the baby's head and add a few of his chromosomes, to stake his claim before the child was born. He did not anticipate Gabrielle putting up such resistance and he never got anywhere near his objective. She pushed him so hard in the chest he slipped and crashed against the taps. In the struggle she lost hold of the telephone, which sank in the bath.

'You prize idiot!' she shouted.

He got out of the bath, taking a look at the telephone receiver lying on the bottom of the tub. At least there was no French left in her now, he had taken care of that.

Gabrielle took his place at the taps. She tried to hide her vulnerability, tucking her knees up under her chin. 'What do you think you were doing, Harry? I didn't know rape was your line as well. What do they call rapists in prison? Peter told me the name … nonces. Are you a nonce, Harry?' She pushed each steaming syllable through her front teeth with her tongue.

'No.'

'Is that the kind of man you are?'

'You don't know what kind of man I am.' Harry struggled to put his suit back on over his wet skin.

'I have an image of you governed by straight lines. Border lines, walls, fences. Within these lines you live in a box, not one but many, like a matrioshka doll. The boxes protect you from ghouls, mummies, spectres – all symbols of death that seem to surround you. That's the kind of man you are.'

The coffee had survived the fight and perched on the edge of the bath. Harry made a big gesture of taking it away from her before sweeping out of the bathroom. He banged the door behind him and dumped himself at the kitchen table, a real banquet slab of oak. A pool of water formed round his bare feet. He looked at the kitchen décor that Samson had paid for. He'd never really noticed how well designed it was. The cabinets had been sponge-painted to create a marbling effect. The walls were maroon, contrasting with the blue Turkish tiles running around the sinks and working-space. On Gabrielle's next birthday, or as soon as he was solvent, he intended hiring another interior designer to paint over the walls, cement on new tiles. Then he and Gabrielle could have dinner parties of their own, like her parents, on a new table surrounded by fresh colours. He looked around once more and Samson's face flew into the same frame of his dreaming. He pulled himself up short and left the flat for the street, where he still belonged.

Harry didn't feel in the mood for working, but could not afford to give in to that. So he toured Kensington Gardens to limber up. Shortly he was lost among hundreds of women in black gowns. They sat in the grass with their faces behind veils, clapping to their children's songs. Hundreds of Arab men circuited the women on the footpaths. They stared cursorily at Harry as if he had no right to be there and conversed sternly with their hands behind their backs. He looked every woman over for handbags, but didn't see a pouch on any of them. He put his own redundant hands behind his back and ambled about, feeling total estrangement, shut out completely from these women's lives.

He went to Knightsbridge to turn a few tricks in Harrods, but the shop was too hot. Harrods' floor security were killers on inflated salaries. He couldn't work in there safely without a firm to shift the joeys around.

Within an hour he was back at Gabrielle's flat, standing outside the front door, penniless, his self-esteem totally grounded. She did not answer the doorbell and so he let himself in with his set of keys.

On the kitchen table was a film schedule for Gabrielle Scott, giving times and scene details, including the location: Goods Way, King's Cross. He folded the paper and wandered in and out of the rooms with her schedule in his pocket, feeling left out, as though he were back in the country again – a lonely boy in his perfect agony, with no human figures anywhere on the stretch of land. He felt frozen in his extraneousness. In the kitchen he kicked the laundry basket across the floor. He needed her drama to thaw him. He took out the schedule and re-read it. He had never seen a film being made. He wondered where they were shooting exactly. A film crew couldn't be hard to find.

He took a cab to the location: the next best thing to making money for dispelling desultory moods was spending what you couldn't afford. The film unit had commandeered an empty factory in the vast desert behind King's Cross. While it waited for property developers, the area was a rendezvous for drug addicts, pushers, prostitutes and film crews. The plumbing hung off the walls of the factory, all the windows were smashed and the floor was thickly carpeted with tabloid newspapers, soft pornography, waterlogged blankets, mattresses, syringes, empty bottles of Thunderbird.

Harry slipped into a corner without anyone noticing him. Gabrielle was centrally placed amidst the debris, dressed conservatively in a pleated skirt and white blouse. She looked ghosted under the strong lights and dwarfed by the dozens of men and women spinning cables around her feet, laying down track. In a way she seemed superfluous to them. Filming was a technicians' game.

An old man burst out from behind a partition and hopped like a scared animal through the people who had displaced him. When he reached the safety of the door he made a passing slur on the industry. 'So this is bloody filming, is it? ... Nobody doing nothing. All that bloody money it costs to make a film and everyone stands around getting paid to do fuck all.' The technicians watched uninterestedly as the old man crashed over the wasteland, stumbling and swearing into the air, then continued with their work. They didn't seem particularly interested in Harry either, concealed in a corner. Their world was the film.

Harry had arrived in time for the third take of a rape scene, which Gabrielle insisted be shot from the point of view of the victim. He watched the scene evolve where a man throws Gabrielle to the ground. As he simulated the movement of rape, Harry formed a square frame with his fingers and isolated her face. Gabrielle was so convincing she made him feel ashamed for himself and for his gender. It would seem only women's lives could be tragic.

The director shouted for a cut and Gabrielle started laughing. It was a huge, echoing, rapacious laugh. She had seen something funny about their activity and had to grip her 'assailant' for support. She couldn't stand up for laughing.

Harry felt duped and stupid, like a card shark's victim. How could she turn emotion on and off like that, like a light switch? With what demonic skill was she endowed? He looked around the place, at technicians' coats and bags strewn everywhere. Inspired by Gabrielle's fraudulent performance he went to work himself and in the same kind of way, with a smile on his face. Anyone who saw him assumed he was benign, a friend of someone else.

As Gabrielle and the crew gathered for another take, Harry slipped out the way he came in. He climbed a wall and lowered himself down the other side to the canal tow-path. He walked east, emptying his pockets, gutting each joey and tossing it into the water. He had made a paltry £25.

Harry ventured home to Marylebone. Without even saying hello to Burgess or Simmy, he took all his suits out of the bosun's cabin. He left, as he'd arrived, without a word.

On their hangers, he hiked the suits over to a quality secondhand clothes store near by called Tatler. The girl who ran the shop looked like she was dressed in her grandmother's lace. Harry asked how much she'd give him for the suits. She inspected them briefly and decided forty pounds apiece was enough.

'You've got to be kidding. Look at the labels ... They're designer names, in case you didn't realize. I paid over six hundred for these suits. Not so long ago either. Forty pounds! That's an insult.'

'Not many people in this area want designer suits.

Perhaps you should sell them on South Molton Street.'

'There are no secondhand clothes stores on South Molton Street.'

'Then I'll give you forty.'

'Eighty. Each.'

'Forty-five.'

'Jesus Christ. I never knew what a thief looked like until I met you. Give me it then before I change my mind. I hope you sleep well tonight.'

'I always do.'

With the only suit he now owned on his back, Harry walked round town, killing time before the evening.

At 10 pm he joined a crowd waiting outside the stage door. As soon as Gabrielle appeared, Harry linked his arm in hers to assert himself. She did not resist him with her admirers flocking round, but turned her face away from a kiss. They climbed into her waiting taxi. Harry expected the privacy of the cab would see a return of her affection, but it only produced silence. She was going to an election night party and seemed indifferent that Harry had attached himself. They sat at distant ends, staring out of the windows as the taxi raced to Maida Vale.

The election party was held in a house, or rather four houses joined together. The producer of the forthcoming *The Merchant of Venice* had linked two terraced houses with the corresponding houses in the next street. The moment Harry and Gabrielle stepped inside she walked off and abandoned him. He wandered around a semi-tropical garden on three levels, partially covered in glass. Dog-sized Koi were suspended in a huge pond as if waiting for work. Keeping vigil over the fish was a blue

marble sculpture of Mary and the Infant. The garden
gave access to the canal, where a 72-foot converted coal
barge was padlocked to a private jetty. The boat was
used exclusively for banqueting and had its own staff
of cook, waiter and boatman, who steered the vessel
through London's waterways while a consortium of pro-
ducers, directors and designers dined off bone china
plates at a teak table, planning their Disneylands for the
West End.

Harry stepped back on the mooring after his tour of
the boat. That was one vessel he *could* live on forever.
All the bathroom fittings were gold plated. An Anglo-
Saxon king holding a book and a sword at the door
guided him back into the house.

Maids and young men in tuxedos walked in and out
of a labyrinth of rooms, carrying champagne and one-
bite crêpes filled with spinach and ricotta cheese. They
minced between uniformly tall models, furniture designers, actors, financiers, investment bankers, television
journalists, newspaper editors, barristers, business con-
sultants – drinking champagne in blue-stemmed glasses.
Over the many heads Harry spotted Peter Samson
working a room with his charm. He was back from his
few days out of town. He also seemed to have *some*
friends left.

In a large conservatory a fifteen-foot bronze god held
arrows of flame over a troupe of African musicians.
They were introduced by a barefoot woman in a silk
dress as 'singers, historians, raconteurs flown in from
Mali just to perform at this party'. Everybody cheered
before settling in to listen to xylophones made from split
gourds, finger pianos, talking drums and an instrument
that looked like a pregnant guitar and sounded like a

Welsh harp. People sprayed the musicians with £20 notes in return for improvised praise songs in a language they didn't understand.

Harry expended a lot of energy wandering around the house trying not to look friendless. In the children's playroom, several television sets were banked up against the wall. Each screen was tuned to a different satellite channel bringing in results from the constituencies. No one was watching, the room was entirely empty.

The party was a prize opportunity for Harry, a well-stocked, police-free sanctuary. He started to gorge himself in a bedroom where people's coats and bags had been left. He pulled a chair up against the door, barricading himself in, then fell on the bed, rifling through raincoats, briefcases, handbags. The people at this party weren't the type to carry much cash around, but he had never seen such a variety of credit cards. Except the cards were useless to him. They would be too old by the morning to sell to a friend like Denis, or even to another fence. Harry suspected he was already on a black list for selling old cards as new down at King's Cross. He took one Visa card, just to keep in shape, then left the bedroom.

For five minutes Harry sat alone in a rattan bamboo *chaise-longue*. Despite his gold cufflinks, his Porsche watch, Yves Saint Laurent silk socks and good looks nobody in the room gave him a second glance. People at the party were like the Hasidic Jews in Golders Green: they could recognize a *persona non grata* when they saw one. Harry expressed his malcontent in the only way he knew. Taking the barest precautions he lifted a joey from a suit jacket abandoned on the *chaise-longue*, then backed off into a bathroom.

He spread his meagre earnings on the floor. He had a few yen, dollars and about £40 sterling. As he sat on the toilet, an actor he'd seen at the party smiled up at him from the cover of a *Vanity Fair*. He kicked over the pile of magazines, British editions of the American glossies, which all had actors on the covers. In the middle of a General Election, it was still actors who sold magazines.

In the kitchen a battalion of Filipino domestics was washing dishes, replenishing platters, opening champagne. Every twenty seconds the door swung open and a maid appeared from a huge cloud of steam, carrying a tray above her head. A parlour table with carved cabriole legs was swollen with food. On a silver salver engraved with horse-drawn barges and butties was a fish so large as to seem part of the human race. Harry promptly sliced a slab of flesh from its belly. He lowered himself into a chair that was perched on ten hooves. He melted the salmon in his hot mouth and stared at the empty chair twinning his own. All around the room chairs had been arranged to promote intimate couplings. The air whispered with their intoxicated conversation. Several people approached the empty chair beside Harry only to peel away at the last moment to take one next to someone else.

Among the reasons Harry gave himself for becoming a confidence man was the desire to be counted by people who would otherwise pay no attention to him. His social failure at the party was made all the more abject by recognizing that same desire in the investment bankers and stockbrokers, licking the salt out of actors' air.

Gabrielle was in conversation with Samson, dressed in a black motorcycle jacket. They sat on twin mahogany chairs styled into Italian gondolas, carved with blossoms and entwined tendrils. People were flocking over to kiss Gabrielle on the cheek and shake Samson's hand. They were both celebrities, he as infamous as she was famous. Some pop composer, who created music tracks for the movies, sat at a Fazioli piano and spontaneously composed a song about the two of them. Samson saw Harry sitting alone on the other side of the room and waved. Harry felt very flattered. He held firmly to the gesture for comfort.

Gabrielle was at complete ease whether talking to artistes or businessmen. Indeed, there was very little in the whole party likely to make her feel unaligned. If any guests weren't rich they were famous and Gabrielle was both.

Gabrielle was the child of the new relationship between art and business investment. Yet barely concealed in a short strapless black velvet dress, its bodice decorated with gold starfish and fake jewels, she looked too wonderful to ever belong to anyone. In that single moment of non-partisan awareness, Harry learnt more about her than ever before and, by the same token, knew he was in love with her. The realization was accompanied by an infusion of physical strength and an emotion hitherto unfelt.

The African musicians finished performing in the conservatory at 2 am. Harry kept seeing them around the house, cornered by tall women in mini-skirts pressing bare suntanned thighs up against their robes, as if they hadn't had their money's worth in the music; what they really wanted was an adventure with a black man. The Africans looked gravely excited. Maybe they thought it was their pay-off, too.

Harry decided to go home at that point. After an

unsuccessful search for Gabrielle, he left. As he closed the front door, the whole house rattled like a snare drum. What sounded like laughter swept behind his back.

At 3 am Harry woke Burgess by climbing into the boat. 'Where have you been, Harry?'

'To a party.'

'You didn't want to take me?'

'You said you never like going out.'

'A party's all right. Was there dancing?'

'Nah.'

'Have you heard the result?'

'Result of what?' he asked.

'The Tories have won again. I've been watching it on TV. Until two this morning it looked like it might have gone either way. Then the map of England suddenly turned completely blue, like it was asphyxiating.'

FIFTEEN

The following day Harry cut across town to Gabrielle's apartment. Something was bothering him, something in their relationship was misfiring. It worried Harry, and as usual when he was worried by something, instead of thinking it through, he went straight to the source with a flushed face and banged on the door. Gabrielle let him in, turned her back and walked through the flat without offering a word of greeting.

'Peter didn't turn up at the boat last night ... this morning,' he stuttered.

'He's gone out of London.'

'Again? Where to?'

'I don't know. He didn't tell me. You and he seem to be hitting it off. Why don't you just ask him yourself?'

Harry went to take a leak in her bathroom. The toilet lid was closed. He unzipped himself roughly and lifted the lid with the toe of his shoe. Gabrielle had been in there before him and had neglected to flush the loo. The water was bright yellow with her urine, discoloured by vitamin B tablets. On the very bottom of the pan was a tampon stuck in the bend and a circle of crimson menstrual blood. Harry examined the aesthetics of the perfect red circle sunk in yellow. Its real significance came home to him as his own urine splashed out. Very suddenly he wanted to weep. That rose of England in the saffron pool now read like his horoscope.

Harry walked in on Gabrielle in the bedroom and caught her around the arm. 'I can make you pregnant for real,' Harry gushed, 'and you'll know who the father is then.'

'I'm not sure I want to be pregnant, Harry.' He felt the walls of the apartment collapse around him like the sides of a wooden box into the shape of a cross. 'I want to be Portia.'

Harry's face was stinging and his ears ringing in the dark. 'How long have you known you weren't pregnant?' He could tell she was smiling in the dark. 'What made you think you were pregnant?'

'The childless woman I'm playing on stage. We began to have a symbiotic relationship. I gave her the baby she couldn't have. That's what happens sometimes when you go deep into a play.'

'Does this change anything between us?'

'Does it change anything?' she repeated. 'What's there to change?' Gabrielle yawned, her large mouth gaping in his face.

Early the next morning Harry leapt out of her bed and dressed in a rush, mobilized with a sudden neurotic enthusiasm for work.

He rushed to Queensway and gunned through Whiteley's shopping mall. He dipped shoulder-bags without covering himself with a newspaper or a coat. He removed cash from the joeys, replacing them empty into the same bags in one unbroken routine. He was wearing his wool Hugo Boss that was too heavy for the warm weather. People looked suspiciously at his perspiring face. Women recoiled as he tossed and bowled along like a man rowing across a tempestuous sea.

Harry was suddenly propelled forward onto his hands and knees by an overwhelming external force. He felt a cold seizure in the back of his head followed by a numbing blackness. His nose began to bleed heavily onto the marble floor. As he was passing out he took a glancing look behind at the three youths in baseball caps and sneakers, steamers all three, who had put out this piece of the competition with a sawn-down axe shaft.

His face crashed forward. Suddenly he was racing with Samson. Samson was running on water, streaking out of sight into the mouth of a tunnel. He turned to smile at Harry, his head framed by the moon of the tunnel mouth, knowing that victory for him was a fore-gone conclusion. What an iceberg he was: cool, glacial, his destructive capability hidden under the surface. He emerged from the tunnel and crawled into the ice ware-house. Harry saw Gabrielle on the tow-path, adjudi-cating the race. She was somebody else now, stranger than any stranger, a fragment of a dream, like air. He tried but couldn't recall a single thing she had said to him, while everything Burgess had said he could remember as if they were his own words. Then the picture went dark, like a moonless night, and his head filled with the sound of Manx shearwaters.

By the time he had reached Gabrielle's communal garden he felt like an old man and a newborn baby simultaneously. He unlocked the gate and walked between the white stucco blushing in the evening sun. It was a little town in heaven, no troubles had ever turned the soil and he was glad to be back. The sun rouged the windows. The foliage of the trees and the grass looked on fire, torched by the sun. Harry stopped walking to absorb this extraordinary vision when a great shoal of pigeons broke cover and flew into his face. A wing clipped the swollen skin on the side of his head and he fell on his knees in the dry grass in a state of shock.

He looked in every room in the flat but there wasn't even a note from her. He felt a chill of abandonment. He wanted to show her his wound, to prove his pain, to demonstrate it wasn't only women who bleed. On the kitchen table was her new purse that replaced the one he'd stolen. Gingerly he checked it over, then burrowed surgically for the cash. It was well endowed with twenties in a dog-eared envelope. He needed to borrow the money – she would understand. He just needed enough for a new suit.

Harry went into a boutique on Kensington High Street and chose a suit off the peg. Using a mirror he admired himself in the metallic grey double-breasted jacket. It was a suit to go to work in. He pulled a plain white shirt off the shelf with a size sixteen-inch neck, a silk tie and a pair of brown brogues and put them all on. He handed over his old suit with the torn lapel and the bloodstains and asked the manager to ditch it. The bill came to £650. He folded the receipts carefully away into his pocket. Gabrielle would have to get to know how much he'd spent just to honour an evening's date with her. If that didn't impress her, then he didn't know what would. He counted his remaining notes before folding them into his pocket. A couple of hundred pounds was all he had left in the world. He had nothing saved, no assets, no nest egg for a time like this. The sensible thing would be to return to work for a few days, but he'd lost the stomach for it.

Gabrielle had asked Harry to turn up at the Café Pelican between nine and nine-fifteen, so she could introduce him to the director he'd first seen at the pond in Hampstead. Their little scam had worked: the director had seen her name on the list of contenders she'd amended and had called her for an informal interview at the Pelican. Why she wanted Harry around to meet the director was far more apparent to her than to him. But Harry wasn't complaining. Gabrielle had a massive collection of friends and colleagues who got more time with her than he did. She explained it wasn't like that at all. Friends were usually colleagues and colleagues sometimes friends. They always combined work and pleasure when they could. It was a complex system. But Harry just wanted to be introduced to some of them.

He arrived at the restaurant at nine. Gabrielle and the bald man with pince-nez glasses were sitting at a table near the back. Harry started to make the long haul to their table with his heart riding up his thorax. They were talking as he got there and he stood marooned, not wanting to say anything to break in. Gabrielle moved her head very slowly towards him, a large smile she'd been wearing for the director toning down into a weak grimace for Harry. 'Hello,' she said tentatively. 'What are you doing here?'

Harry stuttered, 'Come to see you, of course.'

Gabrielle laughed and told him to pull up a chair. They caught a waiter for another glass and Harry was poured some red wine. Gabrielle made the introductions. 'Harry, this is Michel. Michel, this is Harry.'

Michel was wearing a sweater his mother had knitted. It hung off his shoulders like a hairy Gower sheep. Too fond of it to let it go, he wore the sweater with the elbows out. Harry would never dress like that. He couldn't understand why a man at the height of his profession would not want to advertise the fact.

The first thing out of Michel's mouth was 'What do you do?' in a French accent.

'Go on, Harry, you can tell him,' Gabrielle urged.

Harry's eyes and nostrils flared a message to her. My line is not some game. He turned to Michel. 'I do everything, from A to Z.'

'No, Harry, tell Michel *what you do*!'

'He does not have to tell me. I don't mind.'

Gabrielle put on a tragic face that so appalled Harry he barked, 'Well, I'm a pickpocket! Used to be a pickpocket,' he added for safety.

Michel looked startled. He removed his pince-nez glasses and laughed. 'You are serious?'

'Sure he's serious,' Gabrielle said hastily.

She told Harry that Michel's current project was about street criminals in Paris. Then she made him part with the knowledge, trade secrets of how firms worked on the underground, the way they opened and closed carriage doors, confused the punter and took his wallet. He showed Michel his fingernails filed down into points and demonstrated his skill in removing money from a wallet with one hand. Harry took no pleasure from it, beyond the look of ecstasy on Gabrielle's face. She had engineered this 'chance' encounter and would no doubt be reaping the benefits later on. Harry was happy to have helped her career, but not in this way. He did not want all her famous friends and colleagues to be brought down to his level; Harry wanted to rise to theirs.

A shrill ring woke Harry. The red numerals of the alarm clock blazed away at 1800 hours. He had slept through the day. At first he couldn't figure the noise: a tom cat purring? A police siren? The telephone ... Harry waited for the answering machine to pick up the call, until he realized the machine couldn't have been switched on. He decided to ride it out. It would be for Gabrielle, anyway. The caller was so persistent Harry felt he wanted to hide. When he could stand it no more he crawled across the bed, fumbled with the telephone and dropped the receiver off the edge of the table. He recognized Samson's demanding tenor shouting through the receiver, dangling from its cord like a white meatless bone.

'Hello, hello ...'

Harry retrieved the receiver. 'Is that you, Peter?'

There was a pause. 'I expected to get Gabrielle.'

'I've just walked in. She's not here.'

'You've still got her keys then?' Samson cornered Harry.

'Where are you phoning from?'

'From a mobile. I'm on your boat, actually. No keys necessary. Burgess is making me a nice cup of tea.'

Harry felt uneasy on Burgess's behalf. 'Good,' he managed, 'she makes good tea.'

'I'm leaving tomorrow, Harry, leaving England. I've got it all set up. Remember me telling you about my old friend Eddie? The one with the boat? Well, Eddie's come through for me. Can you drive me somewhere down on the south coast? He's taking his cruiser down there and he's going to hop me across the Channel. I've got some other people waiting on the other side to look after me. I'd like you to drive me tomorrow, if you could, Harry. I'll arrange for you to borrow Gabrielle's car. There's a lot of water down there and I'd feel a lot safer if you were around.' Samson's mobile crackled and faded into a thin line of silence.

Harry made his way over to Burgess's narrow boat at Marylebone basin, pulling hard against a gale force eight that had swept into London from the south.

Underneath the ice warehouse he tapped his knuckles against the cabin roof. Burgess came to the door holding Simmy. Over her shoulder he could see Samson in a state of muted fury, trying to fit a bit into an electric drill.

'He's agony on the brain that man,' Burgess whispered. 'I've had to show him how to hold a screwdriver. That's very sad for him, I think. I've never seen a grown man get so upset. He throws temper tantrums, like a child. Do you know he can't even swim?'

He followed Burgess down the boat. She gave Samson the specific task of holding a batten under the gunwale as she rammed home a vertical rib. 'Look at me, Harry … using my hands. The dignity of labour.'

Burgess rolled her eyes at Harry. When Simmy started crying Burgess went to attend to her. She returned with the baby under one arm on her hip and three mugs of tea strung on a finger by the handles. Politely, Samson helped free the mugs and sat down again on a stack of new timber.

'Peter's in the building industry,' Harry injected quickly into the silence. He turned to Samson. 'I don't suppose you've ever had to work with boats before?'

'I used to be a roofer before I started developing property.'

Harry and Burgess swapped incredulous looks. 'If you were a roofer,' she almost laughed, 'then you must have used all sorts of tools.'

'That's right.'

'Then how come I had to show you how to turn a screwdriver?'

'I haven't been up a ladder in fifteen years. I've blanked certain things like that out of my mind. They were bad times for me.'

'Bad times?' she queried.

'I used to get sub-contracted to put the roofs on an estate and not get paid. I'd shin back up the roofs and saw through the beams, destroying my own work.' He looked out of a porthole into the dark catacombs of the building and changed the subject. 'I like this warehouse you're in.'

'I don't live here. I live on the boat, on the longest street in the world. I look out at the canal sometimes and it seems a dream come true.'

'Yeah, a property developer's dream,' said Samson.

Harry registered the silence outside the boat. 'Where's Irish Jack and the others?' he asked.

'They've passed out on the whisky Peter here brought them. He gave them a crate.' She didn't seem impressed.

Burgess went to pee outside the boat. Samson picked up Simmy and sat her in his lap. The baby smiled at him with her fist in her mouth. Harry noticed how her head looked deformed from the back, flat as a clothes iron. If the first time he'd approached Simmy was from the rear, he'd have said the prognosis was going to be bad. But the view from the back belied the charm of her little face.

Harry grinned when Simmy reached out to fumble with Samson's shirt buttons. Samson jerked her away with far greater force than was necessary and held her up in outstretched hands as though examining an X-ray. Harry did not move or make any reproach, paralysed by a fear of contradicting Samson. He took short sharp breaths, as he fought to see Simmy through Samson's eyes – as a thing that was there, just a dumb animal, like a cooing pigeon.

'I had a brother her age when I was about fifteen. He had a shock of red hair and a purple birthmark on his lip. For a couple of years, before he could talk, I had this insatiable appetite for torturing the kid. I just did it to make him cry and seek comfort from me, his tormentor. I'd pacify him until he stopped crying and then do it all again. I was testing my moral limits. How far I could go. I used to get high from it. I got warm in the throat and my hands would tremble and my cheeks burn like I'd been driving very fast.' Blackcurrant jam was spread over Simmy's face. 'Look at that mouth, Harry. She looks like she's been shot in the back of the head.' He shook her until her face grew tense, her eyes widening. 'Cootchy-coo!'

Harry's discomfort grew into fear as he watched Samson tighten his hold on her, the confused tension in her face. 'I let him fall off the table once. I let him squiggle across the table on his back, watched his wee head and shoulders pass the point of no return. He lay still for ages, hanging off the edge, and I thought I was going to burst into flames. My whole face was lit up. Then he kicked out and lifted off, turned in mid-air and crash-landed on the floor.' Samson laughed. 'Sometimes I had to walk away from him, it got so bad. It was like an addiction in the end. I used to wait all day for school to finish so I could go home and work on him some more.'

He lowered Simmy onto his knee, put her nose between his fingers and twisted it around hard. Simmy stared in disbelief at Samson, inhaled the silence, then screamed it out. 'I remember holding him under water for a whole minute. I'd seen this programme on TV about newborn babies surviving in water for forty-five minutes. Joe wasn't newborn, he was one year old, so I just held him down for one minute. He came up with his eyes screwed together and holding his breath. But he never cried. Do you know why babies first cry after they've been born? It's because they take in oxygen for the first time. We're born fish, Harry. We spend the first nine months in an ocean of amniotic fluid. Our bodies are 70 per cent water.'

Samson bolted for the front cabin with Simmy screaming in his arms, leaving a crazed laugh in his wake. He'd squeezed past the engine before Harry even realized he'd gone, then he followed him onto the deck where Samson held Simmy by her arm over the edge of the boat. He looked ready to drop her in the canal like a book he hadn't particularly enjoyed reading. Harry grabbed Samson's wrist, a knot of muscle, rigid as a steel gantry. 'What the hell are you doing!'

'Will she sink or will she float? They say babies can swim, don't they?'

'Don't do that, please ...'

Samson was grinning. Harry couldn't tell for sure if he was being serious. Meanwhile the baby was hoarse from crying. 'I don't see the point in all this – ' Harry was still trying to bargain.

'The point is, Harry, can you go against nature? It's what you have to do to test your courage in our times. What are your limits, old man?'

Samson swung his arm out, as though to fling Simmy into the water. The cabin roof started to chatter with running footsteps. Burgess launched herself off the roof onto Samson's back and reclaimed Simmy in one deft move.

Irish Jack, the Scotsman and the Welshman rained down on Harry and Samson, pinning them to the deck, punching and butting wildly. Harry looked through bloody eyes at the huge, snarling face above his own and felt a crushing depression with who he was. The physical suffering was a welcome way out, his concerns narrowed to pain control. He felt himself grow icy inside, like meat cooling in a freezer.

Burgess was sitting on the gunwale, ripping open her shirt so Simmy could suck on her breast. The baby was too beside herself to drink and Burgess fought for control over her own emotions not to further distress her baby. Irish Jack held Harry by the collar while the others trapped Samson under their boots. Burgess rocked Simmy to and fro and words came out of her mouth like steam. 'I should let them kill you, except you're not worth it.'

'I was trying to stop him,' Harry pleaded.

'You brought him here. You brought him to my boat.'

'I tried to stop him. I'm not like him. We're not the same person ...'

'Well, it sure looks that way to me. You have no right to be a parent again.'

'Again?'

'Are you going to act the blind fool all your life, Harry? Look at the colour of Simmy's eyes. Who do you think she got them from? But you never want to think, do you? About your childhood, the work you do, your future, us. Is Simmy your own daughter? Does it matter? It's an opportunity you've squandered one way or the other, chasing fast money. Stop being a shark, Harry. Try a ... Try being ... like a sea-horse.'

Samson bowed his head to smother a laugh. Harry asked for an explanation. 'The male sea-horse carries the egg, Harry, fertilized in his body by the female. He's one of the most responsible chaps in the sea.'

Harry saw Samson's eyes glaze over. He looked drunk on a cruel atavism. Trying to keep up with this man, adopting his philosophies, had triggered a crisis in Harry only now frothing at the surface. Samson, the man who had it all, was just a nonce. A leaden centre of sin lit up by money. But at the critical juncture Harry proved to be out of his league. He had stopped short of dashing Simmy's brains out. An inalienable nurturing instinct, or maybe sentimentality (he was glad of it), had prevented him going the distance.

Burgess had shown him a better alternative. In a fleeting moment of clarity, Harry recognized that her capacity for unconditional love was what was possible. She had created Simmy who then created Burgess. Parenting had helped her go beyond herself, to test her moral limits – so perversely inverted by Samson.

Harry and Samson were roughly ejected from the boat by Burgess's people. They scuttled out of the warehouse onto the canal tow-path like a couple of rats. Harry felt stranded on a barren plateau with this man. Initially placed up there by his own infatuation, he was now unable to see the way down. Samson patted Harry on the back as though encouraging some promising initiate. Harry shrugged him off, shivering from his touch.

SIXTEEN

Acres of yellow oil-seed rape backed onto pale wheat. Apple orchards, oast houses, emerald-green undulations crowned by single oaks, PICK YOUR OWN STRAW-BERRIES, FARMHOUSE CREAM TEAS passed by. Affluent, traditional, abundant were adjectives with a home there – a museum country in pristine condition. From under the wheels of the car the land stretched in so many incorruptible straight lines. Furrowed brown earth seamlessly phased into grey sky, a dust-kicking wind uniting the two. Irrigation canals cut through black fields in trenches of blinding silver.

The landscape slid across the car's windscreen between Samson and Gabrielle's heads. Harry stung with the significance of being in the back seat. He had been asked by Samson to drive him to the coast. Then Gabrielle demanded to come along for the ride. 'She loves trouble, you know that, Harry,' Samson offered by way of apology. 'And it is my car, after all,' she added. And so it happened that she got to drive and Harry was relegated to his minor role in their lives again. Pensive and tense, Harry was also preoccupied with a harrowing image of Simmy sinking in water. He felt responsible about what happened to her back on Burgess's barge. He had introduced Samson, made Burgess take him on as a lodger. She was unlikely to forgive him that.

Gabrielle's road craft was impeccable. She had kept well inside the law, jumping not a single light nor exceeding a speed limit since the journey had begun in London two hours earlier. Gabrielle had a stash of ready-made joints in her glove compartment which they smoked serially as soon as they got into open country. It was good-quality blow streaked with opium and helped loosen things up between them. Gabrielle giggled and Samson turned in philosopher's evidence: 'This is the Garden of England, Harry, with a golden calf in every field.'

Gabrielle laughed. 'When Harry sees a golden calf, he runs in and steals the milk.'

Samson passed the joint into the back seat and challenged her. 'I was small time when I started out. Harry just needs coaching. Times are changing, Gabby. The act of birth is no longer the most important day of our life.'

'Really?' she sighed. 'Then I guess that puts the spit on the back of the stamp.'

'Simmy ...' The name stuck in Harry's throat. In the past two hours all Harry's clear ambitions had gone to hell. He didn't know why he should be in the back of this car, what he was doing any more. He felt out of his league with these two, out of his depth.

'Who's Simmy?' Gabrielle asked.

'He knows ...'

Samson laughed and snatched the joint out of Harry's hand. 'You've had enough of this shit.'

At a promontory in the extreme south of England the car crunched over shingle and stopped. The sea was right there, the French coast visible on the horizon.

Harry revolved his head to relax the tension, ten times clockwise, ten times anti-clockwise and the landscape spun around with him: marshland, shingle beach and a nuclear power station shrouded in sea mist. Dozens of converted railway carriages decorated with seashells were decaying in the salt air. Not a single tree broke the skyline. Telegraph poles and miles of wire held the promontory together.

Samson asked Harry to leave him alone with Gabrielle for half an hour. Harry granted a runaway's last request and wrested himself out of the back seat. In half an hour's time she would be all his again.

Harry was quite glad to get out of the car and shake his legs. He walked along the edge of the sea away from the car, the loose shingle holding his ankles like traps. Big waves smashed into the shingle rampart, exploding like gunshot every ten seconds. The sea retreated, peeling back a layer of screaming shells. He could hear the hum of the power station's turbines trapped inside the mist.

The sea was very deep at the shoreline. A solitary mister fished in the area where hot water from the cooling towers was pumped into the sea. He stared down his line towards a buoy marking the end of the hot-water pipe. Harry tried projecting himself into his uncomplicated life. But Harry didn't know how to fish. He couldn't do anything recreational, like playing tennis, bowls or golf. He never went to the cinema, museums or concerts. He had only been to the one theatre. All he ever did was work. He leaned against a beached fishing trawler, sheltering from the wind, and gazed back at the car. They were embracing inside. Harry dipped his eyes. Another thirty minutes, he consoled himself. He jumped at the sound of a reel screeching as the fisherman re-cast his lure.

There was no movement, no crowd, nothing happening anywhere. Places like this Harry dreaded most. Empty natural spaces where men could make no mark, where the sea rattled in twice daily in an eternal dreary hell.

Drawn inexorably towards the car again, Harry listened to his feet crunch in the shingle. Oil tankers and cargo ships passed so close to shore he could see their crews moving around on deck. The wind was brisk and silent. He had returned to within fifty yards of the car, when a white cruiser that had been coming progressively closer to shore anchored just outside the line-out of surf. It sat like a swan with radio antennae. Samson's people had arrived to collect him. The cruiser, sixty-odd feet in length with smoked glass windows, had to be a million-pound piece of work. He compared it to Burgess's craft, which had been raised from the bottom of the canal and fitted out for nothing at all.

A small dinghy carrying two men was launched off the side, its bows lifted high by an under-powered outboard. Hundreds of seagulls and oyster-catchers displayed anti-thetical flight patterns overhead. Then the dinghy got into trouble. A set of three big waves caught it broadside, the first almost capsizing it. They sped back out over the top of the second wave and through the feathering lip of the third.

The passenger door of the GTI opened and Samson stepped out. He walked towards the sea, waving his arms and shouting, the words flicked into oblivion by the on-shore wind. At the shoreline he kicked off his shoes and rolled up his trouser legs to the knee. As he waded into the water to his ankles, Harry's first thought was for his suit. The salt water would ruin it. His second thought was for Samson himself, who probably had no idea that in two more steps the shingle sheered off into an eight-foot drop under the water. Harry shouted but his warning was taken by the wind in the opposite direction.

Samson waded deeper and sank completely. A wave lifted the dinghy over its crest, breaking with a long canon-boom, re-formed and sucked the coiled mass of Samson's body up through the trough, slamming him down on the shingle rampart. The sea dragged him back over the pebbles and shells.

The sea never grew old, never grew weak. Harry knew how it worked, its nuances and foibles. Underwater a man could survive three minutes at most. But with large waves steaming you down, the body's store of oxygen is depleted faster. Samson could not swim. Another minute more of this hammering and he would drown.

Gabrielle ran from her car towards the sea, plunging into the water and clutching Samson by his hair. They both sank under a collapsing wave, coming up the other side a moment later. Samson began panicking energetically, flailing his arms. Gabrielle got hit on the head and let go of him to raise both her hands to her face. Another breaking wave flicked their limbs into contortions. Then Harry lost sight of them both.

When your life is being torn away by a force of nature, worldly success is no more useful than loose change weighing you down. In any sea troubled by tides and currents and surf Harry had no fear. He knew how to survive in that unconscionable element. He saw in front of him the kind of opportunity he'd waited a lifetime for. Harry knew he could save them. And by saving them – he would be their champion.

Suddenly he was a force of nature himself, charging towards the sea, plunging off the shingle rampart. The beach was so active, one moment he was in twenty inches of water feeling the rip whore at his ankles, then out of his depth the next, being sucked out to meet an eight-foot wave. The wave dumped on him, pulling him over the falls, down on the stones. His face tore against the shells under the water. His legs were tugged over his back like a scorpion's tail. The sea retreated with a huge deafening roar, beaching Harry on the shoreline.

He spotted Gabrielle struggling to keep Samson's head up out of the water, ducking under the waves that were breaking over a sandbar. They were being swept into the break by the undercurrent. The dinghy could not get inside to pick them up. Harry made his second entry, diving under a wave and pushing on hard towards them. Gabrielle was keeping Samson from drowning by bobbing down underneath him every few seconds and pushing him up to get air.

The surf belted into Harry's face like gloved fists. Water poured through his nose and ears and out of his mouth. Just another five metres or so. He swam with grim determination and pulled Samson away from Gabrielle. The rip sucked her into a wave, smashing her hair into juicy brown forks, and somersaulted her backwards.

Harry lay on his back and kicked his legs, hauling Samson by his arm. He tried to swim under the wall of white water bounding towards them. Its brute force brought both men into a sitting position inside the white kernel of the wave, facing out to sea.

In another few seconds all three were side by side, linked up together, united by mission. Gabrielle was gagging, coughing and belching. The sea was cold and oily, with great coils of spray flying around their ears. Harry's eyes stung with salt, his clothes were dragging him down and he was shivering. He hadn't seen the dinghy for some time now. He shouted but Gabrielle couldn't hear. He wondered why that was when the caw of seagulls was quite audible overhead.

After several more wrenchings by the surf, Harry found the calm beyond the breaking waves. Samson was limp and passive and gave no more resistance. They held onto each other like family, treading water in more stable sea.

The dinghy reappeared, moving quickly towards them. The sea hissed loudly and plumes of spray fell on them like driving rain, each layer cut through by spectrums. The dinghy bounced, its engine idling. Harry saw two pairs of hands come over the side and a face, who he assumed must be Eddie, concealed by aviator's sunglasses. Harry sank beneath the water as he raised Samson under the arms. Samson was pulled out of the sea and flipped over the gunwale. His face reappeared over the side, pale and ghosted. His bloodshot eyes sought out Harry in gratitude.

The dinghy had drifted in a few metres and a large set of hollow waves moved silently towards them. The outboard throttle was twisted open and the craft raced seawards. Samson was on his way. The dinghy climbed the face of a five-foot wave, which sent the craft airborne off the lip. For a second the dinghy held vertically. Samson lay crucified against the rubber floor, his head to one side, arms stretched out, holding fast to ropes.

And in that image all Harry's hopes were raised. He felt for Gabrielle's hand under the water and she wrenched it away.

She began to swim frenetically, but the rip just held her in the same spot. Harry knew that people drowned off-shore by panicking like that, swimming against a rip until they exhausted themselves. The waves go where you want to go. In one direction, to the shore. He wanted to tell her to travel by wave to the shore, but she wouldn't have heard him over the noise of the surf. He seized her arm tightly and waited for the next wave to loom up behind and fold over. He shouted, 'Swim!' before crawling as fast as he could towards the shore. The wave rolled him forward five metres in a mass of white water. Harry broke the surface and saw Gabrielle on his left side, treading water. She was watching him now, trusting, ready to copy his action. Another wave steamed through and they began swimming with leaden arms. The wave lifted and carried them forward. They repeated this until he felt his knees scrape shingle.

He climbed the shingle rampart and dumped himself on dry land in exhausted contentment, anticipating Gabrielle's pleasure as she waded out of the sea. Behind her he could see the white cruiser raise its anchor and turn about, then nose towards France. He saw one man in the wheelhouse, one in the aft and Samson propped against a rail, throwing up into the water. A towel was draped over his head like a boxer.

As Gabrielle approached, Harry raised a hand to her from where he sat on the ground. She walked straight past him towards the car. Harry let her go a little further before following. His feet sank into the shingle. She turned around once and Harry could see her nose was bleeding. 'I have just the thing for that,' he shouted awkwardly, the wind pushing the words back down his throat, shaking his cheeks against his teeth.

She reached the car and opened the door. Sitting in the driver's seat, she pulled in her wet skirt like a fishing-net. Harry heard the door slam and the engine turn over. He swallowed hard and tried to run, but just made bigger holes in the shingle. The car reversed onto the asphalt road. 'Where the fuck are you going?' Harry said quietly. 'Ah, Christ! Don't play games, I'm fucking freezing.' By now the car was almost out of sight. He made a survey of the promontory, gaunt and unyielding, and prayed she'd come back as soon as her senses returned.

The pub behind the power station was empty. Fishing-nets and ships' wheels hung from old roof beams. A fruit machine flashed in a corner. He stood in the middle of the bar, looking at his bare feet, his skin taut from salt drying on his face and his head full of water. There was no sign of a barman or customers, just a noise building up around him, pounding his ears with an incessant urging of some sort. Harry was overcome by sudden and profound hunger. Then he went into a spasm of sobbing, his skin skating around the bone of his face.

The sound in his ears drew his attention to a pay telephone ringing beside the fruit machine. It seemed to get louder and more shrill, the apparatus vibrating on the wall. Harry ran to the telephone before it stopped ringing, his heart on his sleeve, hoping Gabrielle was trying to reach him. He picked up the receiver. There was silence. A female voice asked, 'Is Bernard there, please?'

'There's nobody here ...' Harry vented off a coil of sadness.

'He's not standing between the fruit machines?'

'The bar's empty.'

'If he comes in, could you tell him his mother's here with Mary. She can't get her front door open ...'

SEVENTEEN

For the third time that day his nose began to bleed. He sank to the floor of Peter Samson's Shoreditch bedsit and pinched his nostrils. Whenever he thought about Gabrielle for too long this would invariably happen. He let go of his nose and made a blood sacrifice, shed blood on her memory. He immediately started to feel better, like a woman allowing herself to cry. A breeze blew in through an open window, covering him in city dust and the infirm scents from the prison below.

Several weeks had evaporated since his day at the seaside. After Gabrielle had driven off without him, Harry took eight hours to hitch-hike back to London. He went straight over to her flat and tried to let himself in. But his keys wouldn't fit. Under the door were traces of sawdust. She'd had the locks changed some time during those eight hours.

He went to find Burgess but she and the boat had gone. His possessions were piled up on the side of the basin below the warehouse. She had folded his shirts neatly and returned all his money.

With these few articles of clothing, Harry tramped across to Samson's sentimental home in Shoreditch. At least Samson had not changed his locks. The door gave into the sour-smelling room. Harry crawled onto the sofa and fell asleep for eleven hours.

His throat and nose were clogged with blood when he woke. Washing his face in the bathroom, it occurred to him that all he'd managed to secure from his adventures with Gabrielle and Samson was the illicit use of his bedsit and her nosebleeds.

With the exigence of a mission, Harry hauled himself down to the Vaudeville theatre. In his pocket he had Gabrielle's ox-blood purse. He had never given it back, kept it as a souvenir. Now he wanted to return it, as empty as he felt. He stood in the foyer, swirling a whisky around in a glass, the sound of metal doors banging in his head.

He waited until the interval and burrowed into the auditorium with the crowds. The house lights dimmed, Gabrielle strolled in from the wings. The stage lit up like summer and she began her soliloquy on the Hades of childlessness. He walked down the aisle, planning nothing beyond the next footstep, feeling a thousand eyes boring a hole into the back of his head. He pulled himself onto the stage the same way he got out of a swimming-pool, the same way as he had climbed out of the Hampstead pond onto the raft. For a moment he was sitting on the edge with his feet dangling in space. He blinked against the harsh spotlights, then sprang to his feet, remembering what he was there for, and walked upstage. He pushed an actor in the chest, took his markings and stared Gabrielle in the eyes. Her face was wet with tears, like a drip-dry shirt. At first she didn't respond to the change in actor, too engrossed in being someone else. But then he saw it dawning, with a cold thrill, saw her terror of the unscripted moment. She rolled her eyes into her skull to try to escape him. The audience had accepted Harry now as part of the play, the *dénouement* even. When he gave her a push to see if she'd turned to stone, Gabrielle lost her balance and stumbled backwards. Harry was in a good retributive position, but he couldn't raise one word against her. He was caught up in this imaginary world of hers and could think of no punishment real enough.

He looked into her stony face as though examining a monument. He tried to piece together the jigsaw of her character. There was no one in his experience to whom he could compare her. She was a piece of work, like Samson said. Harry had never believed until too late that he *was* just a distraction for her, a little spot in her life abruptly brushed off, like dust. He had been good material and that was about it. What he overheard her tell Samson had been the truth. Any interest she had shown in Harry held as long as he was doing crime. He performed a decent act in the sea, acted out of character, and lost her interest. Saving Samson's life, even *her* life, was a bromide and she could not get away fast enough. Gabrielle didn't care for lifeguards and abandoned him on a windswept beach.

How had he fooled himself into thinking he could be a part of her society in the first place? His understanding of this was only partial. Like so many people, he'd seen the writing on the wall and believed what it said: money was the new utilitarian culture. At the time of meeting Gabrielle, Harry was raking it in.

Harry had been led by this belief to a closed door, with the people whom he aspired to emulate laughing on the other side. Money had bought him a taste of modern love: that strategic, expedient thing, infiltrated by market forces. Gabrielle made investments in relationships, expected returns. Any love she had shown him was counterfeit. And while she could make passionate pleas for childless women on stage, her understanding was only intellectual. The slow, dull craft of parenting was redemptive, and Gabrielle was easily bored by virtue. 'Actors are their own children,' she had said and faked pregnancy. Harry stared out to where she pitched her nightly laments and saw only hollow blackness beyond the lights.

He stuffed her purse into a pocket of her costume and removed an object already there. He jumped off the stage and walked through the audience who were nodding and whispering to one another.

In the foyer, Harry ran into a couple leaving the box office kiosk. They were hand in hand until something about Harry made them snap apart and stand open-mouthed in muted fear. He looked at his clothes to see if there was something on him, like blood, to have frightened them. In his hand he was holding the pistol he'd swapped for Gabrielle's purse. By an independent will, the gun was pointing at the couple.

Harry heard himself say, 'Your wallet, please.' The man proffered his wallet in an outstretched, shaking hand. Harry took the joey and, for the first time in his career, saw terror on a punter's face. His victims usually discovered their losses with Harry out of sight. Now he could see for himself the distress he caused. It was the first time he had resorted to violence, or what seemed like violence in the punter's eye. It made him feel nauseous. He rushed out of the theatre into the Strand, plucking the credit cards and the cash from the joey before throwing it on the ground.

He did not stop until his chest pressed against the Embankment wall, down from the Strand, on the Thames. The pavement was filled with tourists, eating bags of roast chestnuts, come to be near the great river. Warming themselves on vendors' braziers were young and old men, huddled together under grey blankets. It was raining gently on them.

Gabrielle's personal prop was still in his hand. He offered the pistol to one of the men lying at his feet, down on his luck. 'It's only a toy,' the guy said, and gave it back. Harry told him who it belonged to, but the man had never heard of the actress.

Tourists encouraged the pigeons with scraps of bread and they kept landing on Harry's head, digging their claws into his scalp. The men lying on the ground stared up at Harry holding his toy gun, with pigeons climbing over him, and thought of him as one of their own. He was offered a drink from a bottle of Thunderbird, tendered a cigarette. Harry rejected their charity to look down the Thames as far as it allowed. Tugboats cut each way, boastful as drakes. Lightermen stood statuesquely on gunwales, oblivious to life on land, to the tourists, to Harry. The post-modern buildings on both sides of the river made promises they couldn't keep.

Harry turned the pistol in his hand and smiled at the thought of Gabrielle, who at any moment now would be reaching in her pocket for it and taking out her old purse instead. She would have to kill herself somehow with a joey. The only form of punishment he could think of inflicting was to steal her means of self-destruction, so easily rectified by the next performance.

He locked up the bedsit and walked along the canal with an eye to selling a few credit cards to Denis. At Maida Vale he broke into the toilet cubicle and, while waiting for Denis to turn up, snorted a couple of lines of his cocaine off the blade of a kitchen knife. Harry had never bothered with drugs before. Denis had cut the cocaine with Johnson's baby powder, which irritated Harry's nostrils. Once more his nose dripped blood. He dug into his pockets for tissue, but he hadn't carried any for some time. He searched all the drawers for toilet paper. He sprang open a cabinet on the wall filled with coffee jars, sugar, milk. The milk carton rattled. From the carton poured a shoal of little coloured capsules. He didn't know what they were but ate a handful before stepping outside.

From the moment his eyes settled on the water the canal seemed to speak to him: come with me, out of yourself. As long as he remained within sight of water he felt he still had options. Where there was water there was hope. He walked on to Marylebone. The sun bounced off flanks of smoked glass, halfblinding him as he groped his way under the ramp into the ice warehouse that had preserved Burgess in safety for so long. She had not returned, the basin was empty. The water seemed forlorn and miserable without its guest. It had lost its muscle and become slothful and stagnant again. The vaults were also silent and grave. The three Celts had gone too, the cobblestone path littered with empty bottles and the cold embers of their wood fires.

Outside the warehouse he stood under the raw

materials of a developer's vision of the future – copper, steel, glass, marble, granite – and felt impotent. He found himself thinking about Peter Samson as his nose dripped little pin-head spots of blood on his shirt.

He walked back along the tow-path. The canal surface was scuffed by a wind that blew his nosebleed dry. Outside Denis's toilets he lay down and stuffed his hands into the canal. Turquoise and green dragonflies, the colour of Gabrielle's eyes, skimmed the surface of the water.

He tried to stand and his legs crumbled like pillars full of termites. He fell on the tow-path, water frothing by his nose. He tried to lift his face off the grass and released a gale of disapproval in his head. The grass was blood red, the sky pink as flesh.

He crossed various thresholds of sound until the thunder in his head grew more distant. Cupping his hands behind his head he tilted his face and saw that he was naked. Blood splashed his pallid flesh. His head spun three times clockwise, detached itself from his shoulders, then drifted off across the canal, its spinal cord trailing in the water. Burgess appeared, steering *Irish Jack*. Black leather shoulder-pads of her donkey jacket shone in the sun. Simmy was strapped into her cot on the roof. Burgess stretched and grabbed Harry's floating head by the cord and handed it to Simmy, who held it like a balloon on a string.

He vomited, spraying his jeans with half-digested capsules. Behind him were the toilets. He felt for his head, which was very tender, but where it should be. There was no barge on the canal, no Burgess.

He curled up on the tow-path and found Denis poking among the capsules he'd vomited. 'You been at my

Ecstasy? That looks like fifty quids' worth you've just sicked up. Jesus, look at you. You look like today's news. You need a fucking wash. Hup! Off you go.' Harry felt the weight of a boot placed squarely between his shoulders and he rolled off the tow-path into the canal.

He descended through varying layers of cold in total darkness until his hands touched the ground. In the soft bed of the canal Harry clutched at something intriguing. He closed a fist around a yielding object, like a hand. Was this the hand of Domino Waunarlydd? The man who loved the canal, who had been around during its last days as an industry, who died because he wanted to live in the past. Did Samson really have him killed or was he merely trying to pump himself up?

Harry opened his mouth and let the water pour in. He felt a new life beginning, a return to return. If he could just remain submerged for another few minutes. He began to feel the cool and oily water coursing through his body. The canal inhabited him and he began pleasantly losing his inhibitions. The same image stuck in his mind, of his own head floating in the air, Burgess catching it by the spinal cord and giving it to Simmy to hold like a balloon. He was so happy, so very fortunate to feel this connection with Burgess and Simmy. It was all he really desired – his family, who preserved the old traditions of love beneath an erstwhile ice warehouse.

He had a good thing going with Burgess before scampering after what glittered and lucking-out on fool's gold. She had offered him respite from the grief of solitary acquisitive routines. He had never appreciated the quietude of that relationship because the emotion was antithetical to those which fuelled Samson and Gabrielle's ambition, ambition with fell purpose.

Revivalism was taking place within him. Drowning gradually, he was visited by another vision, of himself stretched out in the bosun's cabin of Burgess's ark, his hands behind his head, Simmy sitting up in her cot, both watching Burgess draw ley lines in pencil across an ordnance survey map. The boat's fittings had been completed and they were moored in country. An easy silence hung between the three of them, tinted by a seraphic flush of violet from the early morning sun.

Harry stuck his chin out, rising through the darkness with the last of his strength. There was only one watery highway they could possibly be travelling on. He could easily find them. He broke the surface of the water, holding on to this connection with Burgess and to what he believed was a piece of the Welshman in his left hand.

His eyes full of water, he sought out familiar landmarks: council flats, tunnel, public conveniences, Denis. In the new light of resurrection, even Denis looked beautiful, tattooed to the hilt. Corseted by water around his chest, Harry raised his arms like an evangelical, palms out, ready to receive the nails. In his fist was not the hand of a Welshman, but an empty joey – a pickpocket's trophy. He threw it at Denis's feet, who jumped back quickly, unsure of what it was. Harry began to laugh with a resonance he'd lost for a decade or so. A deep vaulted laugh that poured out of his mouth like dust.

Discover more about our forthcoming books through Penguin's FREE newspaper...

Penguin
Quarterly

It's packed with:

- exciting features
- author interviews
- previews & reviews
- books from your favourite films & TV series
- exclusive competitions & much, much more...

Write off for your free copy today to:
Dept JC
Penguin Books Ltd
FREEPOST
West Drayton
Middlesex
UB7 0BR
NO STAMP REQUIRED

READ MORE IN PENGUIN

In every corner of the world, on every subject under the sun, Penguin represents quality and variety – the very best in publishing today.

For complete information about books available from Penguin – including Puffins, Penguin Classics and Arkana – and how to order them, write to us at the appropriate address below. Please note that for copyright reasons the selection of books varies from country to country.

In the United Kingdom: Please write to *Dept. JC, Penguin Books Ltd, FREEPOST, West Drayton, Middlesex UB7 0BR*

If you have any difficulty in obtaining a title, please send your order with the correct money, plus ten per cent for postage and packaging, to *PO Box No. 11, West Drayton, Middlesex UB7 0BR*

In the United States: Please write to *Penguin USA Inc., 375 Hudson Street, New York, NY 10014*

In Canada: Please write to *Penguin Books Canada Ltd, 10 Alcorn Avenue, Suite 300, Toronto, Ontario M4V 3B2*

In Australia: Please write to *Penguin Books Australia Ltd, 487 Maroondah Highway, Ringwood, Victoria 3134*

In New Zealand: Please write to *Penguin Books (NZ) Ltd,182–190 Wairau Road, Private Bag, Takapuna, Auckland 9*

In India: Please write to *Penguin Books India Pvt Ltd, 706 Eros Apartments, 56 Nehru Place, New Delhi 110 019*

In the Netherlands: Please write to *Penguin Books Netherlands B.V., Keizersgracht 231 NL–1016 DV Amsterdam*

In Germany: Please write to *Penguin Books Deutschland GmbH, Friedrichstrasse 10–12, W–6000 Frankfurt/Main 1*

In Spain: Please write to *Penguin Books S. A., C. San Bernardo 117–6° E–28015 Madrid*

In Italy: Please write to *Penguin Italia s.r.l., Via Felice Casati 20, I–20124 Milano*

In France: Please write to *Penguin France S. A., 17 rue Lejeune, F–31000 Toulouse*

In Japan: Please write to *Penguin Books Japan, Ishikiribashi Building, 2–5–4, Suido, Tokyo 112*

In Greece: Please write to *Penguin Hellas Ltd, Dimocritou 3, GR–106 71 Athens*

In South Africa: Please write to *Longman Penguin Southern Africa (Pty) Ltd, Private Bag X08, Bertsham 2013*

A CHOICE OF FICTION

Summer People   Marge Piercy

Every summer the noisy city people migrate to Cape Cod, disrupting the peace of its permanent community. Dinah grits her teeth until the woods are hers again. Willie shrugs and takes on their carpentry jobs. Only Susan envies their glamour and excitement – and her envy swells to obsession... 'A brilliant and demanding novel' – *Cosmopolitan*

A Good Man in Africa   William Boyd

'A highly accomplished comic novel, uproariously funny, but also carefully constructed, canny, and artful' – *Observer*. 'A wildly funny novel, rich in witty prose and raucous incidents ... without qualification, a delight' – *Washington Post*

Los Gusanos   John Sayles

'Savvy and savage ... a broad and impressive portrait of the last fifty years of Cuban life' – *Washington Post*. 'There is a score of characters in *Los Gusanos* ... each has a story to tell, and Sayles tells them all well ... a vivid read ... exciting, sexy and humorous' – *Independent*

Lantern Slides   Edna O'Brien

'Superb ... Her stories unearth the primeval feelings buried just below the surface of nostalgia, using memories to illuminate both what is ridiculous and what is heroic about passion' – David Leavitt in *The New York Times Book Review*

The Woman's Daughter   Dermot Bolger

'A novel of enormous ambition, an attempt to create a folk history for those whose dark sexuality has banished them into the underworld of their own country ... a serious and provocative work of fiction' – *Sunday Times*